The King's Pawn

By Aaron Hanania

⟁ The King's Pawn

Dedication

I dedicate this book to my family members and close friends who helped me through the seemingly-endless process of writing a book.

My father, Ray Hanania, was a huge driving force in completing this book. He helped me extensively to finalize and edit the final product. My mother, Alison Hanania, always inspired me to higher achievement towards perfection, and honor. I also want to thank my sister Carolyn and my Grandmother Darla for their love, support and inspiration.

I owe a huge thank you to my friend Dan Hickey who helped bring my crazy vision for a cover page to life, and several friends including Sean who read the initial draft and helped me keep a sharp edge on the story. And I want to thank my high school English teachers whose classes made writing for me fun and helped change my outlook on life.

In writing this book, I wanted to share my belief that anyone can achieve their dreams if they try. I am proud because this is the start of my dreams which continue to expand. I hope this inspires other young people from my generation to follow their dreams to wherever they may lead. Don't allow a stumble, a mistake or second thoughts to prevent you from always reaching higher, doing better or going further towards your goals.

Finally, I want to thank Steve Jobs. We never met, but his iPhone technology and design became my sole writing instrument, my silicon-diode typewriter, in composing this entire novel.

The King's Pawn

The King's Pawn

ISBN   978–1–387-79157-6

First Edition Published by Aaron411.com

Printed in the United States by Lulu.com Press

For all general information about this book, please contact the author by email at TheAaron411@gmail.com, through his website at www.Aaron411News.com, his YouTube Channel at www.Aaron411.com, or by snail mail writing to him at P.O. Box 2127, Orland Park, Il., 60462.

Artwork for this book was designed by Dan Hickey

Prologue

Growing up, life was seemingly perfect for us. Every single aspect of life was perfect. Every number was even, every time was even, everything was square, never imperfect.

We were young and we were not aware of the irregularity of life. I never realized the oddity of our situation.

We woke up the same time every day, had the same schedule every day, yet nothing bad ever seemed to happen.

Each day was a perfect runover of the previous. What made life so difficult for us was the sheer perfection and meticulousness that we lived in every day.

We lived in a way that made us think that we were the only society and that other ones did not exist. Nobody knew the real truth because nobody had ever ventured out of our society, which was surrounded by a tall structure that was too tall to get over.

Everyone in our society was very monotonous and showed very little emotion towards their daily lives. That was another factor that made life tough, nobody showed what they believed, so it was hard to enjoy life because nobody was emotional.

I had a few ways to enjoy life and speaking to my sister was one of those ways. We liked to play games with each other and talk about how our day was; a great way to pass time.

As it turned out the oddity of the format of life was the least of our worries.

Chapter One

The alarm rang every two seconds starting at 6:00 A.M for two minutes exactly.

Every morning of the week started out with the exact same alarm at the exact same time. Following the alarm, I would get out of my bed and take a shower for exactly five minutes. I would not spend a second more than five minutes under the tepid flowing water.

My sleeping quarters had one bed that was always made perfectly, and two square windows, which were 18 feet wide, that faced the street. I loved to look out at night.

My closet was always quite tidy because I didn't have many clothes; our educational uniform was a white short sleeves t-shirt and blue khaki pants. Both boys and girls wore the same uniform.

In our life, everything was very uniform. I viewed life just like a clock, the eternal ticking, that was never offbeat, was the eternal perfection of our "cyclistic" life.

My parents both worked six days of the week. On the last day, which was called the Gifted Day, they both remained at home with my sister and I.

My father's occupation was at a gargantuan facility. He did not talk much about what he did, so I did not know much. He always woke at 5:00 A.M and left the house at 6:38 A.M. He was never late, not one time. It goes to show that everything functioned perfectly.

My father had short, straight brown hair, not beige, not dark brown but neutral brown hair. Everyone in society had a solid hair color never a mixture. It was a detail lost over time, just the same way a name is forgotten over time.

My hair was black like my mother's hair. Her hair, too, was straight, but longer than my father's hair. My hair was never below my ears, because for a boy to have hair below the lowest point of his ears was against The Code.

Speaking of which, The Code was the groups of laws that everyone obeyed. They were very strict rules that kept our society running without any problems. For females, according to The Code, hair mustn't be above the bottom of the ear. My sister's hair was long enough to touch her shoulders. She too, had the same brown hair as my father.

Our house was on a block with ten houses, each of the same shape, size and color. Houses in our society were not called houses but rather "Location of Origin." I always called them "LOO's".

Our front lawn was a perfect hue of green, because according to The Code, "Any quantity of private owned property with a lawn must never be a color other than green and no more than a one-half of an inch in height." If someone broke that rule, they could be arrested or have their house condemned, so people did as they were told.

The LOO's on each side of the roadway were solid white in color. They were square in shape, the same as the ones on either side. The only exception of a LOO being unlike another is in the case of the head of society, the Chief Elder. His LOO was just a bit larger than the rest, and was also the only LOO that was not in the shape of a square. Nobody could ever figure out why, but most members did not put any thought into it anyways.

Every morning at the same moment of time, at 6:45 A.M, my sister and I walked out of our LOO. The white paved path extended fifteen feet to the white sidewalk. There were ten trees in front of the LOO's, one per LOO. Our LOO was four plots away from the corner which had not a rounded edge, but that of a right angle.

The Education Bus picked up four youth at the corner of Street A and Street F, which was our street. Our society was regulated according to The Board of Elders -- the members of society who set standards and regulations and had the power to revise The Code if necessary. The Council deemed "youth" as any member having less than eighteen years of life.

The Education Bus was a solid yellow, square vehicle with four wheels that took the youth to the Education Center, the EC. The Code broke EC into four branches. EC1, which was for ages 4-7. EC2 was for ages 8-11. EC3 was ages 11-14 and EC4, ages 14-18. My sister and I were both in EC4.

The Education Bus came at exactly 7:00 A.M. every day. It was never late, never. Our EC was eight minutes away from our stop. The driver of the Education Bus always drove the same route to the Education Center. He always drove at the same speed. I always saw the same members walking and driving, because every day was a mirror of the previous day.

I don't remember a time that was unlike the other times. The Education Bus dropped us off in front of our EC at exactly 7:08 A.M. We, the six youth, had to walk exactly one hundred steps to the front of the Education Center. In our branch, EC4, there were one hundred and twenty five youth. In total, there were six hundred youth in the program.

Education started at 7:30 exactly. Each room had twenty five youth and every day, we sat in the same seats. The seats too were symmetrical perfection just like everything else. There were six rooms, each with an Educator. We called the Educators the teachers. The teachers came to us, the same time every day. The only item of our day that was different from the previous, was what the teachers spoke to us about. I was always interested in the concept known as history.

In society, members could not have any ambitions, because there was a big ceremony to choose an occupation. It was a process that I was unsure of the logistics. I knew however that a member had no role in what occupation they were given. But I had an ambition for history that I had to hide from the other members.

I secretly researched history because I found deep interest for it, and it was the only thing I really enjoyed. I had to keep my research secret because The Code prohibited "Any external research or information from being maintained." It made no sense, because I could not see why The Board of Elders did not want the society to find out information about themselves.

I had a neutral interest for every other topic in Education, because each day was basically the same. We had a break for thirty minutes exactly, a time when we could obtain nutrients. It occurred at midday. The time in which there is a transition between the two halves of a daily cycle, Morning and Evening.

Another part of The Code that made Education a bit less interesting was the rule of interaction. It stated that, "Any interaction between peers in any form during the Education time from 7:30 until 1:30, is punishable at the discretion of The Board Of Elders, Educators, or Head Educator." the Head Educator was an elderly man who lived next to the Chief

Elder. The Head Educator was in control of any changes in Education or problems, which were very rare. I cannot recall that an incident had ever happened. He was also in charge of punishments, and he was strict I heard.

That is why I didn't have too many acquaintances, because youth could not interact. The only youth I interacted with on a regular basis, was my sister. She was the only member I could be with outside of school and speak to.

Education terminated at 1:30 in the afternoon. The youth walked to their Education Buses to be taken to their LOO. The busses departed from the EC at exactly 1:50 in the afternoon every day.

My sister and I did the same thing after Education every day, we did our Extra Work, work that was to be handed in the following day. We got the same amount of extra work every day. When we were finished, we were able to play simple Time Users, things that were used when one had extra time from the day. I loved having extra time because I had the ability to do one of a few things, so we had a choice. We could do what we wanted to, of course, following the rules of The Code. We usually just talked about concepts like philosophy.

Mom and dad got home the same time, 6:00 in the evening. I am unsure of what my mother did for an occupation, because she never told us either.

When my parents came home, I called our LOO home, because in Education I remember the word home being a place of one's origination at the end of a day.

I would ask the same question every day,

"How was your cyclistic frame?" Cyclistic was a synonym for the word cycle.

My mom and dad would both say, "Son, today was ok." they never used adjectives, nobody did. The only reason I knew what descriptions were was because Education told us when we were little. When my sister and I spoke, we rarely used adjectives, because things were simplistic and nothing was unusual.

My favorite day was the Gifted Day. It was the only day that we could do what we desired, while still obeying The Code. Our family often went out to an eatery and had food. It was alright.

I noticed that everyone around us seemed lifeless, and had no emotions. I don't think they knew what emotions were. I knew I had emotions, but I made sure others did not know. I could tell my sister had emotions too, but not my father. Again emotions too, were a very important detail that I overlooked.

Chapter Two

My father was driving our white rac. A rac was a four-wheeled automated vehicle. We had two racs, my mom had a white one and my dad a large blue one. The LOO's were passing us by. The rac in front of us came to a halt.

"Mother, why is our world so perfect?" my sister asked.

"Honey, just imagine if our world was imperfect... you would not like it, would you?" my mom replied. I could not answer because I had never experienced another society.

"I think that would be better because nothing new happens here," my sister said.

My mother's face went from normal to flabbergasted. I had never seen her react like that. For many years she had kept her emotions hidden from us.

"Honey! You must never exclaim that again! Never ... if anyone heard you say that, you would be condemned!" my mom said forcefully and worriedly.

"Well I say what I believe," my sister said. That was the first time anyone had ever acted abnormally.

"No no, why shall I be in charge of this youth!" my mom mumbled under her breath.

She turned to my father and said with a raised voice, "Honey to the Condemning Station... NOW!"

She seemed very angry about what my sister said, but I could not figure out why. I had never seen my mother expressing anger, or any emotion really.

"I think you just broke a rule," I said turning to look at my sister.

She looked back at me. "I just wanted to say what I believe," she said to me.

"Why are they so mad?" I asked her.

She looked unfazed and replied, "Because you know and I know... they don't and they are just doing what they have been told to do."

"Why are we the only people who seem to have a mind?" I asked my sister sarcastically and rhetorically.

"I have thought about that too, it's like we are the only real people or something," she replied in a joking way.

That was when I noticed the video object as we were passing it. They were in many places. They too, I overlooked.

"We are going to the Condemning Station!" my dad said angrily.

Chapter Three

Location - Unknown

A man, half asleep at his monitors with his coffee in hand was the first to notice the camera. On his screen he saw the one thing he hoped to never see … "Dispute Sector 2"…

He jolted nearly out of his seat, perplexed by what he was seeing. The camera showed a white car driving with four occupants inside. There were two kids, a boy and a girl in the back of the car. The man driving seemed upset, but the woman in the seat adjacent to the man had a tiny, very tiny phone in her hand, that read "DS2."

The man got out of his seat and turned to the worker to his right and said, "John, John … Come look at this tell me what you think."

"I swear Derek, if you're wrong you're dead, I am so tired of your false alarms from Sector 2. The boss isn't happy when you cause chaos for no reason," John said.

John was a middle-aged man about age 40, he had a wife and kids. He was employed by the government of The United States of America. His assignment for the last fifteen years was the main cause of conflict for the country. It was in the eyes of every other country cruel and inhumane. The one goal... see what a regular human would do in a situation where everything was perfect and they had unlimited power.

The whole week was a cycle. The two humans under testing were the two children, the boy and the girl, known as the pawns. The woman who had the phone was also a regular person who was aware of the experiment. She would actually drive to the headquarters of the project and report her views. The father was not aware, nor were any of the other people. The experiment was known as "The King's Pawn."

John looked at Derek's screen and froze. He saw the phone in the woman's hand that read "DS2".

"This cannot be real! Not here, not now... Why me? Why me?" John questioned.

"That is what I said. What should we do?" Derek asked.

"You need to raise the alarm, only you have the code," John said.

"Alright... they won't like this because every other alarm has been false," Derek said.

"If they don't believe us and this whole thing fails it's on them...not us," John said. Derek agreed.

"It cannot hurt to be on the safe side," Derek replied as he began issuing the alarm.

Derek sat back down in his oversized reclining seat and opened a new tab on his Automated Devices that allowed him to type a twenty five digit code. He had it committed to memory after the first week. This code set an alarm off at the headquarters, which was less than a mile from the security building in which John and Derek worked every day.

Derek picked up the wired phone while he was typing the code and called someone.

"Sir, yes it is Derek from S, I have a possible catastrophic situation in Sector 2." A few seconds later he continued, "Yes sir I will raise the alarm. Code Purple."

At 8:27 P.M. on October 21st of 2034, the first Code Purple was issued for the "King's Pawn" experiment.

Location- Headquarters

A middle-aged woman was giving a speech about the benefits of situational research, when she stopped abruptly. She was wearing a tailored suit, with nice shoes and a very expensive diamond watch with her name engraved on it. She had light brown straight hair. Her name was Susan King and she was the head of the "King's Pawn." She was known all around the world. It was a love-hate relationship, half of the world loved her, the other half hated her. She was in Boston, Massachusetts at a convention where some of the world's most renowned researchers and doctors were meeting.

"As you can see, the results of this could change ... Sorry something came up, I have to leave I am very sorry," Susan said to the huge crowd. They all started talking amongst each other very confused about what was happening.

At the same moment, Susan King ran off the stage where her manager was waiting. Susan had an earpiece in her ear that her manager could communicate over. Her manager had just told her "Miss King, we have a code being Issued by a Derek from Security... Importance 11/10."

Susan understood that any code is a bad thing and that it was the most important event in her life, because her manager did not joke around when it came to serious situations, and neither did Derek.

The crowd was still confused as to what happened, but they were told by the emcee what happened.

Susan and her manager were escorted out of the convention center to their awaiting motorcade of black SUV's. When the motorcade began moving, Susan immediately grabbed her Apple Mac from the arm rest and opened Skype.

"My sincerest apologies Mrs. King, but it appears as Sector 2 is reporting an issue, a severe one," Derek said over Skype. The two could see each other on their devices. Susan did not particularly love the small cramped security building that the two men were in.

"Tell me more, I want to know everything," Susan said. She was taking in every word Derek said as if it were the last conversation she had, because it would be one of her last if what Derek said to be true was true.

"Yes ma'am. Our insider from Sector 2, the mother of the children, has reported that the Pawns are rebelling and possibly have discovered they are different," Derek said.

"I never thought this would happen!" Susan said.

Derek was unsure what to do about the situation.

"Ma'am I can only be approved from you, what do you want me to do?" Derek asked.

"Derek just wait, nothing too bad could happen, at least I don't think... I think we wait and see where this goes and then act if we need," Susan said.

"Yes ma'am I will wait. We are monitoring the situation, would you like me to connect you to our screen so you can see the monitors?" Derek asked.

"Of course," she replied.

There was a large screen in the security building where fifteen men and women worked for the "King's Pawn." The screen was to be used for meetings and emergencies like the one they were facing. The face of a tired and worried Susan King came up on the screen. The main screen was surrounded by about 30-40 smaller television screens each showing a different angle from inside the "King's Pawn" society.

"Hello everyone Susan King here. I was just told of a Code Purple regarding the Pawns. I am canceling the code only because this is the first time it has happened. An experiment is all trial and error, this is an error, but it is not worth canceling the project we have worked on for years," Susan exclaimed.

"Yes ma'am, what should we do if something else comes up ... Something ... worse?" a woman said from behind her Automated Devices.

"I am to be notified immediately despite the time of day or night. I am in charge of you all and everyone inside the dome, so if anything arises, anything at all, call me immediately!" Susan said forcefully.

"Let's watch this and see where it goes," Susan said.

Chapter Four

The Condemning Station was exactly four minutes away. The condemning station was a place where a "rebeller" was taken. A rebeller was classified as a member of society who disobeys The Code, it was very rare in our society for The Code to be disobeyed because everyone was perfect, or so it seemed they were.

We arrived at the condemning station exactly four minutes later. My parents parked the rac in the one unoccupied space.

"Out now!" my mom said angrily.

"Wait no please," my sister said, nearly in tears.

"You chose to disrespect both The Code and us, your parents! I never thought that something this … this imperfect would happen with my own child," my mom said in disbelief.

I got out of the rac rather nonchalant in relation to the situation. My sister broke an unspoken and spoken rule … that of respect. The Code states, "Any action showing direct or indirect dishonor to one's parents or guardians is heavily punishable." my sister, by arguing with our parents, showed disrespect, so that's why they reacted as they did.

"Mom why, I am sorry!" my sister said, she was crying by that time.

At that point, my mom, who was most likely very embarrassed, was dragging her child into the Condemning Station.

"You are not sorry. An apology is a false representation to avoid an unwanted conclusion. Your unwanted conclusion is being Condemned … Maybe you will re-evaluate your actions," my mom said to my sister.

"But I didn't mean to disobey," my sister said.

"Maybe this will teach you to think about your actions before doing them," my mother said.

My dad did not seem fazed at all, he seemed as if he did not realize the scenario. The other members of society were walking at a normal pace, not fast and not slow. It was like they didn't even know we existed.

My mom and my sister entered the station, which had a large object with a direct representation of the connotation of the Condemning Station. It read in large solid red print "Condemning Station." The front of the station was the same white as the LOO's, but the station had two large oval transparent frames, called windows. The interior had a white floor, very clean and perfected.

My father and I followed about ten steps behind my mother who was still dragging my sister.

As they approached the desk with rounded edges, a rare sight, the secretary smiled.

"What would you be in need of assistance for?" the secretary asked with a voice that had no emphasis at all. She sounded like most people, neutral, monotone and void of emotion. Her suit was buttoned, evenly and exactly, as protocol dictates.

My mom replied with more emotion than the secretary.

"Yes ma'am, my youth here has shown dishonor for her parents."

"Ok ... Do you want her condemned?" the secretary asked as if she did not care about anything. She did have to work on the Gifted Day, a sacrifice nearly nobody was willing to make.

My mom must have said something to the secretary that I did not hear, because the secretary replied.

"Alright ma'am," she said to my mother. She turned to my sister and said, "Miss, right this way please."

The secretary got out of her seat in one movement and walked around the front of the desk. She grabbed my sister's hand and escorted her out of the main area. The sign above the door said "Intake."

As my sister was being taken away from us, she turned back and had the look on her face as if she had been betrayed. She looked desperate, unaware of what could happen. I felt horrible, but I didn't want to cause a scene.

"Alright honey let's return to our LOO," my dad said emotionless.

We walked back to our white rac and drove back to our LOO. I had to find out what was going to happen to my sister. I was worried what would happen.

"Mom, what's going to happen to her?" I asked. My mom knew that I was talking about my sister.

"Well I wanted her to learn that she needs to be very careful. The reason is complicated, but if she is not careful the result could be very bad," mom responded.

"It is bad, very bad because she is at the Condemning Station on the Gifted Day," I said.

"Things could be worse for her, she is only staying for a short while, or until she has changed her reasoning," my mom said.

"What should I do because my sister is gone?" I asked.

"Just get your thinking away from the topic and think of the daily regular tepid weather. Just act normal please do it for me," my mom said.

"What do you mean to just act normal... everything is normal as it is," I said. I was very confused.

"No it is not honey, not at all... it is complicated but now is not the time!" my mom whispered to me.

We got home a short while later. I like calling my LOO home because it is our home. It is where I feel safe.

The next few days were literally the same as the previous with one exception ... no sister.

It seemed like a part of me was missing ... her hidden personality was gone and I missed it. The whole situation got me thinking what is wrong with our situation. I needed to explore a little and read and do research all without anyone knowing. The only day for that was the Gifted Day. I knew I had to be careful.

The entire cycle of time represented as 1 out of 52 or .01 of a year went by without a sister. I knew that I was in control of myself and only I could be responsible to find out. I did not care what was going on, or even if I was condemned it did not worry me.

Oddly, my mom had to go to her occupation on the Gifted Day. My dad also went to talk with an acquaintance... he had no "friends", nobody did. A friend was only read about, but nobody knew what having a friend felt like. I always wanted to have a friend, but we couldn't. I managed to have one person who was close to being a friend, and it was my sister. She was the only person I was allowed to talk to. We kept our "friend" status hidden to everyone else, just as a precaution.

The Hall of Knowledge is where the books were located. In history, structures with books were known as libraries or bookstores. Books had different stories, some were of truthful information, others were entirely fictional.

I left our LOO with my cycle, each youth had one. Mine was blue, solid blue. I knew the first place to go was the Hall of Knowledge, it was the only place where I would not seem suspicious. A lot of society members went to the Hall to search for topics because our society had a very little amount of technology. The hall was one of the only locations in which "Automated Devices" were available to us members.

On my ride to the Hall, I passed the same symmetrical LOO's and went on the main road with the only store. Society members did not go to the store often, because they only needed seven cycles of clothing because each week was the same. Over time details from society became a blur of motion and life. Everyone took things for granted, everyday things including the sky, the same members walking... it all became a blur of detail that goes unnoticed.

I arrived to the Hall of Knowledge and I knew I was at the right structure because the Hall was unique to our society in appearance. It had two circular towers in the front and seven windows, not six or eight. The interior was filled with straight lines of books, of which each had an even amount of pages, keeping with the symmetricality.

I was not looking for a book, but rather to use the Automated Devices. I had to figure out what was out of place, because I knew something was odd but I couldn't pinpoint what that oddity was.

Chapter Five

Location- Security Building

A week has passed since the first incident occurred with the female pawn. The two workers at the security building had not reported anything since the last incident.

Derek and John were on their shift on Sunday, which was known as the Gifted Day in the dome. Derek was talking to John about topics unrelated to their job. The two had a lot of down time and became good friends. They functioned like brothers, they played cards and had fun, but they always did their job. Derek was monitoring the many security camera angles that were live from inside the dome. One of the cameras showed a young boy riding a blue bicycle on the sidewalk. A few minutes later, Derek noticed that the boy, who was actually the second pawn, was entering the library which was named the Hall of Knowledge inside the dome. Derek had always been against renaming everything in the dome. He thought it was too confusing, a rac instead of car, LOO instead of house, the list goes on. He never found the time to mention to Susan how confusing it was.

Derek knew that the event unfolding on the screen was definitely of importance, but he second guessed his logic and decided not to report the situation. It was John who happened to notice the event.

"Hey Derek, why is the male pawn going to the library?" John asked.

Derek who knew about the situation, but was dozing off in daydreams, responded being caught off guard. "Oh, I am not sure. I don't think it is a threat or of any importance."

"I think you are wrong, because last week the pawns were trying to find out about their society when the female was put in the Condemning Station. You need to report this, because her brother may be trying to research what's wrong with their society," John said. He knew that if something happened in the dome and they did not report it, they would be the first questioned.

"I never thought of that, John. You make a good point. Who shall we contact?" Derek asked.

"I think we go to Headquarters, because they are in charge. Susan does not need to be disturbed ... yet," John said.

Derek proceeded to pick up the same wired phone and call the Headquarters.

The second in command answered the phone, because any call is directed to him, especially from the security building.

"Commander speaking ..." the Commander said.

"Yes sir, it is Derek from security," Derek said. He was interrupted by the Commander.

"I have the ability to read the phone number of the incoming caller, I know who you are. Please get to the point," the Commander said. He did not like to waste time.

"Sir, I am requesting you put the camera from Main Street and the library live on the monitor," Derek said.

"And why would I do that?" the Commander asked.

"Sir, it is because the male pawn is currently at the library on an Automated Device. It might be a good idea to monitor what he is searching, because we think he is starting to realize what's really going on," Derek said.

The Commander realized why Derek called at that point. The boy was trying to find out about the situation.

"All right. Derek nice work... we are monitoring it live," the Commander said.

He turned to his notepad which had "King's Pawn" written on the top and wrote "Susan move John and Derek from the security building to headquarters... right next to my office."

Everyone at Headquarters was able to see Derek's monitor. He zoomed in on the screen of the Automated Device the boy was using.

The Commander ordered a command from his assistant.

"Get King on the phone this instant! She will want to see this," Commander said.

"Yes sir," the assistant responded. She did as she was told.

Susan King was relaxing at her home when she was called. This home was in the city closest to the experiment. It was the largest on the street. It was not too late in the day, so she was not sleeping, but nevertheless she did not want to be bothered, as it was Sunday. She was actually reading a magazine, one of her favorites. She grabbed the ringing phone, which she disliked the ringtone of.

She looked at the caller ID and saw that it was from the Headquarters, so it was an important call, that she had to answer.

A female voice, that of the assistant was the first to break the silence.

"Mrs. King, at request of the Commander, I have contacted you directly to connect you to the Commander," she said. There was a small clicking sound as the girl connected Susan to the Commander.

"Ok, what is the news?" King asked.

"King it's Commander," he said.

"Very obvious," King said.

"As I speak, the boy is at the library using one of the Automated Devices," the Commander said.

"What is the importance of that?" King asked. She was a bit upset at this point because she thought the Commander was calling to tell her that the boy is on the computer.

"It's not the fact he is using the Automated Device, but rather the topic in which he is researching," the Commander said.

"And what would that topic happen to be?" King asked with an attitude.

"He is trying to find out more about the world. Questions like "How many days are in a week? Where am I?"" Commander said.

"Oh ... How long has he been on the Automated Device for?" King asked. She was put on a loud broadcast so everyone at headquarters could hear her voice and she could hear them.

"Mrs. King, about 45 minutes. He is currently still on the Automated Device," an official said.

"We have created the Automated Devices to give false search results to the user. Not only for the pawns but for any other person in the experiment," King said.

Someone started talking but King interrupted them abruptly.

"As I was saying ... There are some faults in the system. Some were implanted purposely and others unpredicted. With those flaws come real world answers, answers that if discovered would quite literally cause a contamination of our results, terminating our project. You are to monitor every letter that boy types until I arrive! Am I clear?" King said firmly to emphasize her point.

King put on better attire than she had on, because she wanted to look halfway decent. She quickly brushed her hair and headed out the door. She went to her car, a tiny red Prius and realized she forgot her phone inside. She ran back into her house and grabbed her cellular phone, not noticing the security card which doubled as her ID sitting on the table.

When she got in her tiny car, she realized how long it has been since she drove a car, over eight years. Luckily she only had to drive about fifteen minutes to the headquarters. It was getting on the premises that was her main concern, because her red Prius was not registered in the system. She would have to figure it out.

Fifteen minutes later, maybe a bit more, Susan King arrived to the complex. The complex was the property that was very secluded that housed the headquarters, security building, the one where Derek and John worked. There was another group of buildings for other workers who create and add scenarios to the experiment.

The main entrance had plenty of measures in place to keep the complex protected. Car barriers, x-ray devices, Electro Magnetic Pulse machines and a fair amount of cameras and other things. Nothing slipped past the security. There was one time when a bird flew over the fence and was disintegrated on spot by accident.

The guards were inside the tiny hut stationed outside the gate, which was made of steel and was electrified.

As King pulled up in her tiny car, the two guards stood up and walked to block the path. They were well armed with machine guns, a taser, and a frag grenade, just to be prepared for the worst.

"Hello, my name is Susan King, I am the head of the King's Pawn," Susan said.

By that time the two guards were on the driver side and in front of her car. The male guard was the first to talk. They both wore military uniforms. Ones that were different from that of the country's military.

"I am afraid you have no permission to be on this property, as the sign said 'No trespassing.' This is government property," the guard said.

"Well that's great, I need to be inside the headquarters because a rather bad situation is unraveling this minute," Susan said.

"Great, I don't care and I can't allow you to enter. You don't have an ID so no enter sorry too bad so sad lady," the guard said in a comical way.

"I have my ID right here, and watch your mouth little guy," Susan said angrily. She hated being mistreated. She went to grab her ID from her purse when she realized it was at her house.

"I left it at home," Susan said.

"That's what they all say," the guard said.

Another guard added sarcastically, "yeah, the masses who get here."

Susan was already calling the Commander to get clearance. The guard did not know why she was calling someone.

"Hands up... Now! I have the permission to fire this gun," the guard said. Susan did as instructed, just as the Commander answered the phone. Susan put him on loud speaker so the guard could hear.

"It's King. I'm stuck at the gate with a clown who is denying my clearance," Susan said. The Commander was upset by what Susan said.

"If you, Tony, don't let her in, you will be fired and taken off the radar permanently," the Commander said.

"Oh, my bad sir, I didn't ..." the guard started to mumble.

"I don't care what you say, I care she is let in!" the Commander said interrupting the guard.

He let Susan King enter the complex, but not before the Commander finished his last statement.

Susan was already speeding through the complex by the time the Commander said his last statement. She was driving quite erratically. Susan was the only one to hear the sentence. Susan was very worried that her experiment could once again become invalid. She was thinking that something was not being done right, because this was the second scenario in the time of one week.

It took Susan another few minutes to get inside the headquarters. She parked her little red car very badly. She was in such a rush that she didn't realize she hit the side of the car parked next to her... again.

"Someone's not going to be happy... I'll leave them this note," Susan whispered to herself.

She grabbed a tiny sticky note that read "Susan King was here."

The Commander was caught off guard by a sprinting Susan.

"Wow you got here fast," the Commander said.

"That's what I do when I find out my entire career could be ruined forever! You would rush too," Susan said.

Everyone was looking at Susan in a weird way. Nobody had ever seen her running, and just all over the place.

"You need to replace those guards. Make a protocol or something because that was an awful experience," Susan said to the Commander.

"My apologies Dr. King. I will deal with it," the Commander said. He would clean house after their meeting.

Susan went to her office to put her stuff down. She noticed a note on her desk. She went back to the main room of the headquarters where the people monitored the live feed.

"I'll give Derek a call, but more importantly let's figure this situation out," Susan said.

On the main screen, the boy was still researching different topics.

"Has he found any flaws yet?" Susan asked.

"Currently he has not found any, but we can tell he is trying to find them," a random worker said.

"Why did I come again?" Susan asked.

"Because we need you here to make the call and give orders if necessary, because none of us have the power to," the Commander said.

"Since nothing too horrific is happening right now, I will call Derek," Susan said.

"If anything happens, do not be afraid to interrupt me. You made it sound worse than it is right now," Susan continued.

She walked into her office and made the call. Her office was very elegant, the way she liked things. It was like her second house.

Chapter Six

Location - Security Building

Derek and John were still monitoring the live feed, when the phone rang.

Derek answered and was surprised when he heard the voice of Susan King.

"Hello Mrs. King," Derek said.

"Hello Derek, please put me on loud phone so John can hear me."

Derek pressed the speaker button on the wired phone that seemed to be historic.

"Hello Mrs. King," John said.

"Hi John," Susan replied.

"I wanted to call you myself to tell you that you have been promoted to Headquarters. We have an office for the two of you. We think that you deserve to be promoted. You are to come to Headquarters as soon as you can," Susan said.

John and Derek were both flabbergasted by the promotion. They never expected the head of the project to call them.

"Wow ... we aaarrrrre so honored! Thank you!" Derek said.

Susan hung up right after they responded.

"Dude we just got promoted!" Derek said.

"I know!" John said.

The two workers gathered their things and literally were out the door they had entered and exited through for the last handful of years. Not that they had many things ... just some photos of their family and other trinkets.

They drove to the headquarters like two children going to a candy shop.

Susan was in her office awaiting any important happenings when Derek and John arrived.

On her Automated Device, Susan had a live feed from the main entrance to the headquarters. Both Derek and John were trying to use their ID card to enter the building. Their ID cards were registered to the tiny security building and not the brain of the entire experiment.

"Show your identification cards please," the automated female voice said to the duo. All Susan had to do was click one of the many buttons on the sound pad that cued the automated voice. She liked having a custom sound pad, one like what musicians use, because she was too lazy to hit a tiny button. She preferred to hit the drum pad with her entire hand. Nobody questioned her odd ideas, because she was in charge.

Derek and John showed their ID cards to the small camera.

"Access denied," the automated robotic voice said.

Susan was at her desk chuckling. She had a hidden desire to mess with people.

"Why? How are we denied? We just got promoted to here!" Derek exclaimed as if he was confused.

"I'm messing with you, the door is open. Welcome to your new office," Susan said through the tiny microphone.

The two men walked to the third level where the main offices were, and that of Susan King.

They went directly to Susan's office. Her door was closed, but the sign with two chess pieces was all they needed.

"Enter," Susan said from inside.

"Welcome to the Headquarters!" Susan said proudly.

John was frozen in awe admiring Susan's miniature palace. Her office had a full kitchen, a living room, television, and meeting room. It was bigger than most high-end apartments.

"Thank you... yes this is my office not my house," Susan said. She could tell what John was thinking from his emotions alone.

"Let's get to the point as to why you are here, as you probably know," Susan said. The phone on her desk started to ring. It was one of the old models, it still had a cord attached to it. The government used phones that were landlines because those were not easy to bug or hack.

"If you would excuse me for a second," Susan said.

The two men patiently waited outside of the office for Susan to finish her call.

"You have a guest waiting Mrs. King. It is the mother from the Dome," the secretary said through the phone.

"Okay send her up, I will be waiting," Susan said.

"Sorry gentlemen, we have an important guest. You will find your combined office two doors down from mine. Let me know if you like it. I'll check back on you later," Susan said.

Chapter Seven

The guest arrived in a small white car. The car was perfectly cleaned. The lady driving, the mother of the two children, was entering the complex where the entire operation is run. She pulled to the gate and was approached by two guards.

"Hello ma'am," one of the guards said.

"Hi, I am Amy, the mother of the pawns," Amy said. It was the first time she used her name in a while because she was always called mom or honey.

"Ah yes go ahead to Headquarters. Have a splendid day," the guard said with a smile.

Amy arrived to the Headquarters and was met by the secretary at the front door.

"King is awaiting your arrival. Right this way please," the secretary said. She escorted Amy to the third level where the main room of the building was. It looked like the air traffic control room from NASA, the American space program.

Amy was not used to the emotion people had in their voice because everyone in the experiment was emotionless.

"Hello Mrs. King," Amy said. She knew that this meeting would be one of the most important because a lot has happened in past week.

"Ladies and gentlemen, please welcome Amy," King said loudly. Everyone turned to look and became silent.

"Hello everyone, I have a lot of information that could help us during our tough time," Amy said.

Susan gave Amy a microphone so everyone on the level could hear her voice easily.

"Thank you," Amy said.

"So, first things first... recently, I have noticed a big change in my two children. They have become more aware of things, more curious, more determined, more everything. I have reason to think that they may know something is very odd about their life. I think that my son has just realized he needs to find out the truth. I think we need to add some more variables to change the experiment," Amy said.

"Ma'am I agree, but how could we change the experiment without intervening?" Commander asked.

"Very simple, since everyone in the system has been brainwashed, it would be very easy to add new rules or other thing without them knowing. Since they have no knowledge of anything but what they know to be true, a new person would not be noticed," Amy said.

"When would we do this?" the Commander asked.

"Soon, but not too soon, we need to get ideas together as to what to include," Amy said.

"Anyone have ideas?" the Commander asked loudly. He wanted everyone to hear him.

"Um yes, I have an idea," someone said.

"Could you please stand up," Amy said.

The short middle-aged man stood up from his work station.

"Yes, my idea is from an experiment done on a group of college students," the man said.

"The Stanford Prison Experiment of 1971?" Susan asked.

"Yes, precisely," the man responded.

Amy, Susan and the Commander were all wondering the same thing. They all asked the same question almost simultaneously.

"And why would we build a prison?" they all asked.

"We don't. We should test the power of the human brain ..." the man said.

"I think that right now is not the right time to make a change since we are getting results," Susan said. "We will know when the time comes, trust me we will," Susan continued.

Chapter Eight

I was trying to use the Automated Device to add to my knowledge. I had a feeling something just seemed odd. I was occupied for two hours at the Hall. One of the numerical values I looked up was the number that I read about. My mom let me read one of her own books and they were different from the others. I remember reading numerical values symbolized as "odd." I typed the numerical value "13579" because I wanted to obtain more knowledge about them.

I was disappointed by the results. There were no results that were an abnormality. I did not want to obtain excess knowledge or bring extra attention to myself, so I decided to return to our LOO. I really did not want to return.

I biked along the same roads, past the same buildings. The only difference was the people, they were not the same as when I first came.

When I entered our LOO, I noticed that my dad had returned because his rac was on our land.

"Hi father, how was the Gifted Day?" I asked.

"It was well son. How was the day for you?" he asked with an emphasis on "you."

"I went to the Hall of Knowledge to read some books and obtain knowledge," I said. I had broken a major rule, I lied.

"How did you obtain knowledge, it is a restricted action?" my dad asked.

"I accessed the Automated Devices in the technology wing," I said.

"Of what topic did you obtain knowledge?" dad asked.

"I um, I was obtaining knowledge about the Gifted Day," I said, I lied again. I realized how disgraceful I was behaving. "I wanted to look back to how it originated."

"Where is mother?" I asked.

"She is returning your sister to us," my father said.

My sister had been at the Condemning Station for an entire 1/52nd of a revolution. I hoped that she would reconsider her actions after being granted a very rare chance, a second one.

My mother walked into our LOO with my sister following closely behind.

"Hi sister," I said. I was feeling happy to see her again. I rarely had a good emotion.

"Hi brother," she said enthusiastically. She seemed rather pleased to return to society. She wanted to hug me, and I did too but we both knew we should be modest. I had a secret curiosity as to what she did for the time she stayed at the Condemning Station.

After she greeted our father, she went to the second level of our LOO. I followed her to where the sleeping mats were.

"How was your stay?" I asked her.

"It was really, really bad. I was questioned about so many things and I could not figure out why," she said.

"Wait... what did they question you about?" I asked.

"They asked about society and The Code. They also asked about you, and mom and dad," she replied.

"Which members of society are you referring to as 'they'?" I asked.

"I am unsure. I could only hear their voices, which sounded monotone," she said.

I was trying to assume the reasons for her questioning. Members of our society do not ask questions unless they are of need. I decided I should consult my mother.

"I think mom may know," I said.

I went to the eating room, where my mom was reading a book with no representation.

"Mother, what did my sister do at the Condemning Station?" I asked.

"Well honey, I am not sure," my mom stated. She looked worried, which was unusual for her.

"Why did they ask her questions?" I asked.

"Oh, why I am unsure," mother said. I noticed that she responded very quickly, as if she was not expecting my question.

"They were concerned about her. The Occupation Ceremony is looming in the near future. They wanted to find her niche in society," my mother said. She sounded nervous and unsure about what she was stating.

My mother looked past my right shoulder in a determined stare, almost frozen. She quickly returned to her place. I reacted and looked in the same direction. I saw our cooking room, everything that has been in our LOO as long as I could remember. There was a very small circle near the intersection of the two walls. A very odd shape in society, a circle... It almost looked like the eye of a bug, focusing so intensely at its prey in the midst of day.

X   The King's Pawn

Chapter Nine

Susan King was still at the Headquarters. After her guest left the premises, she had the time to check on her newest associates. Derek and John were very content with their new office. They had the best Automated Devices money could buy, excessively large chairs and unique imported Italian granite desks, with dark, handcrafted mahogany wood. Susan had anticipated to promote the two long ago, so she had an office built and she waited for the right time to give them the call.

Their favorite part of their new palace was that the entire wall was a television screen, so they did not have to stare at their Automated Devices, but rather the wall. The wall was to the left of the entrance, but at an angle in which it was convenient for the two to look at. They also had a bathroom, very well built, a bedroom for breaks with a closet, and a small kitchen. It reminded John of Susan King's office, but just a tiny bit smaller. The two could now spend more time working because they had all the amenities needed and then some.

They were watching the wall when Susan entered. She wanted to check on the two workers.

"Hello guys," she said as she walked into their office without knocking.

"Hello Mrs. King. Is there anything you need of us?" Derek asked. He was following his natural politeness and his role on the job.

"No, I just wanted to see if you guys like your office," Susan said. She knew they loved it just by their faces. They looked like two young children in a candy store.

"We love it! We are so honored to be here, you have definitely made a proper choice," John said.

"I know... I thought you would like the interior and the new wall," Susan said.

"It makes our job much more productive because we can both see the screen at the same time," John said.

"Plus we can stay here and rotate on and off shift and not need to go home," Derek added.

"I thought you guys would like the little gift I have here," Susan said.

She hit the button under the light switch and the wall opposite of the monitor wall opened up. It revealed a pool table that had different chess pieces engraved into the wood.

"Wow! I was wondering what that button did," Derek said.

"Yet you did not feel like pressing it to find out... oh the irony!" John said.

"I figured you could have a little fun, after all you have worked like dogs for many years," Susan said.

"Thank you so much," they both said at the same time.

"You should only thank yourselves, as you did the hard work and were rewarded," Susan said.

She left their office, which was more like an apartment and headed for her own.

"Wow what else is there here?" John asked as he looked around the room.

"I am not sure, we have to be careful to be on our highest guard, as we cannot get carried away by this new office," Derek said. He was the more work driven of the two, he always worked then had fun.

The two men were able to watch the footage from their office and the rest of the people in the main part of the floor could also see some of the live feed.

John and Derek were hired to provide around the clock watch of the stream. Often, they would make their own shift, changing every twelve hours. Now they did not have to worry as much. Their families understood that their job required a huge amount of hours for a decent pay. They each earned a fair amount more than the average businessman. Their new office which had a large bedroom served as their new home. Their pay would be increased as their hours would be, but they still could have breaks. Over the fifteen years, the two men made a small fortune for working with the government. They both knew Susan before she was appointed head of the project.

Chapter Ten

Over twenty years before, the name of a then inexperienced Susan King was heard by many.

Susan King, born Susan Kingston grew up in a suburb of Honolulu, Hawaii. From a young age, Susan found the brain mesmerizing. Perhaps her father, Leon had an impact.

Dr. Leon Kingston started his career as a clinical researcher. He had a PhD in many medical fields, including clinical medicine. He became a member of the Center for Disease Control, when one of his associates recommended him to the CDC board of applications. He was chosen to be head of the medical clinical research department. He rose to fame when he found a potential cure to Alzheimer's. He made millions from his work, well deserving of the fortune.

When the head of the CDC was going to retire, Dr. Leon took advantage of his opportunity. He wrote a lengthy letter to the head, asking the head to look into his own background and possibly to appoint him as the successor of the Head of the CDC.

The head did exactly as asked and appointed Dr. Leon Kingston the new head of the CDC. His daughter at that time was a normal high school student. Her father's new position allowed her to find more information about the brain, because after all, he worked at the CDC. Her father moved the family to New York City because commuting from Hawaii was extremely difficult. Dr. Leon was given two assistants who would help him and speak for him if needed. John and Derek were assigned to Dr. Leon three weeks after he became the new head of the CDC.

Over the years, Susan researched many things about the brain. Her favorite study was the Stanford Prison Experiment of 1971. The experiment tested the idea of what happens when you put good people in an evil place, will the evil place win? It intrigued Susan because she could not figure out why the results were so different than logic.

Susan went to Cornell University in New York where she studied psychology and philosophy. Her father was a major aspect of her studies, because he knew a lot about the brain. By that time, Susan was trying to get a PhD in psychology.

Susan was playing chess, one of her favorite on the spot inference games with her father, when she got the idea.

"Dad, is testing and experimenting with humans legal today?" she asked.

"Yes, it is legal, but there are so many strict regulations," Dr. Leon said. Susan was ecstatic that human testing was legal, because she wanted to do a test, a big one.

"Why are you asking honey?" Dr. Leon asked.

"When I get older, I want to do an experiment on a family put in a perfect place with extreme regulations and see what happens," Susan said.

"There are regulations, for example preliminary vaccines are tested on individuals who volunteer to be tested. That is human testing, but it is safe … to an extent," her father replied.

"Dad, I am not asking about regulations, I am saying I want to do a test where the setting has extreme rules," Susan said.

"Oh, I see what you mean. It would be a chance of about one millionth of a billionth of a percent anyone would allow that," her father said.

"Well at least there is that one instead of zero," Susan said optimistically.

Susan would spend the next two years in school, and on the side creating her experiment. Her degree was going to be useful when she proposed the idea to the government, because if anyone was granted permission, a psychologist would have a higher chance. She talked with her father many times and got his ideas added to the mix. The only thing she lacked was any other opinions from other doctors and scientists.

May 15th

It was one of the most important days Susan had ever lived to see. It would be the day she showed her idea to the world... well not her, her father.

The father, daughter duo had agreed that her father would bring the idea to the Committee at the CDC, the people who approve and deny research ideas. Susan would join her father who was at that time nearing the end of his working age.

"Committee meeting, May 15th. As I say your name, please say 'present'," Dr. Leon said to the committee, that he was the head of. He read a list of names, his being the first. By the end, three of the forty-two were missing.

"Our first discussion will be of a proposal from myself," Dr. Leon said.

"I am proposing an experiment that will be revolutionary... the first human test in the last decades ... The Kingston Experiment," Dr. Leon said. He would explain the details of the experiment, but the whole idea would be voted against.

Susan did not give up at the failure, she waited and made new improvements to her idea and three years after the first meeting, she tried again.

During the time in between the attempts, Dr. Leon became sick and was in the hospital. He appointed his daughter his successor as the new head of CDC. He kept his position for a while, but three weeks before Susan would stand in front of the U.S. congress, Dr. Leon Kingston died at age 78.

She was the head of the CDC, just a few years out of college. She had a lot of weight on her shoulders as the successor of her father who made many improvements. She had to continue her father's legacy and carry the family name.

Chapter Eleven

Susan was prepared for her speech, more than any other she had ever written. She knew that this would be one of her only chances.

"Ladies and gentlemen, please welcome Dr. Susan Kingston, Head of the Center for Disease Control," the announcer said.

Susan walked out onto the stage while waving at the crowd.

"Thank you for allowing me to speak to you."

"During my life, things were not too easy. My mother died when I was two, and my father worked hard all of his life. Dr. Leon Kingston, was the man who found the cure to Alzheimer's, a neurodegenerative disorder that killed the brain slowly and horrifically. As his daughter and successor, I too want to do great things. I have a potentially revolutionary idea; to test the human to show the power of the brain. I want to prove or disprove logic, and possibly even propose new concepts never before seen to science. The Kingston Experiment, would take a family of four and put them in a literal perfect place. Through neuro-reprocessing, the volunteers would be flushed of any knowledge and experiences and put in our experiment. They would be taught from scratch to follow a very strict set of rules. This would test to see what does supreme power cause someone to do? How would one react over a long period of time?" Susan explained.

"I will now be answering questions and concerns," Susan said.

"Dr. Kingston, how much would this cost?" a congressman asked.

"About two hundred million dollars sir as of right now," Susan replied.

"How would you get the funds needed for such an experiment?" another person asked.

"I have sponsors who would be ready to pay any amount to be associated with this," Susan replied.

"And what if this all goes wrong? Would there be repercussions?" someone else asked.

"Life is full of failures; science is all cause and effect. If you change one variable here, what happens there ... That's what this is all about. We are trying to discover what we do not know," Susan said. "It's not about what would go wrong it's about analyzing what would go wrong."

"Very well then ... How would one be a part of your experiment?" someone else asked from the crowd.

"We would offer the family of a volunteer a one million dollar upfront bank deposit. And over time with interest they would receive around ten million dollars," Susan said. "The bank we found is offering a tremendous interest rate."

No further questions were asked. Quick and concise was the way Susan liked for things to run.

"Ok, we will now vote. All in favor of The Kingston Experiment, say aye," the Speaker of the House said.

The vote was against the experiment, only by one vote. Susan was so close to quitting, but she did not.

"Proposal. If I were to get another country to approve the research under their name, would I be able to conduct the experiment here in the U.S.?" Susan asked. "As it seems that you are not in favor of being responsible for the experiment."

"A vote is needed. All in favor of The Kingston Experiment being conducted on United States territory, but mandated by another country, say aye," the Speaker of the House said.

The vote was in favor for her proposal. After six hours of deliberation, the Kingston Experiment would be conducted in Nevada, in a flat desert over 90 miles away from the nearest major human population. Susan was thrilled, because she just had the biggest moment in her life. It was the first time her experiment showed any chance of future survival.

After traveling to fifteen countries, Susan King's experiment was accepted by the United Kingdom, by the Queen.

"I like this idea, it may be a marvelous program, that I would be glad to sponsor," said the Queen.

Susan was so excited to be able to finally start planning her experiment. She knew it would not be an overnight thing, because of the sheer scale and requirements. The first step was getting volunteers and finding the two children needed.

Chapter Twelve

Susan needed to find people to work her experiment, but she could not figure out how to find responsible people.

She was relaxing at her father's estate that she inherited. She loved the Victorian Manor that was built in the 1800's. The elegance of the whole property stunned her, each room was totally different from the next. The estate was a staple of her family's success.

One month had passed since the Queen agreed to the experiment. Susan needed help and she came up with the idea that would be crucial to the process.

She picked up the phone and called the CDC, because it was the weekend and she was off on the weekends.

"Yes this is Susan, I need to talk to John," Susan said. She appointed her assistant John to her office when she was off. Derek she assigned as her right hand man. She loved the diligence of the two men who would do anything to get their work done the correct way.

"Hello Doctor King. Please dial one if you need security, two if you need a laboratory, three if you need an assistant, and four if you need John," the automated voice said.

Susan dialed the number four and waited for the ringtone.

"Hello Dr. King, John here."

"Yes John, have you got yourself a recorder or a fast hand?" Susan asked. He knew that she was about to tell him lots of information, so he grabbed his laptop to type notes on. He typed much faster than he wrote by hand.

"I am ready ma'am," John said.

"Alright ... I think that we need to offer a pay to any scientists or doctors involved in this. I want Cynthia in PR to get a press release out by tomorrow. It needs to say 'help needed for revolutionary experiment, one million dollar pay, call for more information.' I do not know who you want them to call, but they should call. After that we will go around to the cities and talk and hopefully get volunteers. Their families will get a lot of money because we will put the one million in a bank so it gains interest. I think we need to go to the homeless and other people that would have reason to give their life to science. Can you do that?" Susan asked. She knew it was a lot to ask for at once, and realistically a lot of it would not happen, but she figured she should ask anyways.

"Yes for sure. I will call Cynthia right now and tell her what you told me. The entire country will know by about Tuesday... so in two days from today," John said.

"Perfect... Now we wait," Susan said. She hung up the phone, just as she started to smile.

Tuesday

Susan knew that the day had come for her to unveil the experiment to the country. She flew to the capital, Washington D.C. where she would talk to a large convention of doctors and scientists. The news and media from all over the country sent their representatives to film and cover the groundbreaking feat.

It was the idea of Cynthia to organize a spur-of-the moment convention, because she thought that more media would cover the event, and she was right.

Susan was to begin to speak at exactly noon. It was two hours before when Susan arrived to the large convention hall. Her car was surrounded by media and photographers. It was the first major public reveal of her experiment. Many news channels aired the flyer that Cynthia made in preparation for the convention. It gained worldwide attention literally overnight.

Susan was a very busy woman who dealt with a minor case of claustrophobia. She told her driver to ask the media to form a space so she could talk without feeling uncomfortable. She did not have a real security guard yet.

"Excuse me. Could you please form a walkway so Dr. King can talk to you guys? She's claustrophobic so please respect that she is taking time to do your interviews. Thank you," the driver said.

The media did exactly what they were told to do, because they did not want to ruin the chance to interview Susan King for the first time. It would be the biggest news story in the last few years.

Susan stepped out of the black Lincoln wearing a black suit and very expensive sunglasses that had her name engraved into them adjacent from the large O emblem. She looked like she was ready to tackle anything that came at her.

"Hello guys, thank you for being here," Susan said to the media. Her driver stood next to her as she did her interviews, just to be safe.

"I have exactly a half an hour to do interviews with you, so please do not waste all our time," Susan cautioned.

She started taking questions from the reporter closest to her car, and then slowly moved down the line of journalists towards the entrance.

"Dr. King, what inspired you to make such a large leap in human experimentation?" a reporter from Los Angeles asked.

"You know, I was inspired by my father. He was the reason I sought an interest in the brain. Also, the Stanford Prison Experiment of 71' had a large impact here. I want to test what people really are like and what they will actually do," Susan said.

"Dr. King, what is going to be the toughest part of this experiment?" another reporter asked.

"I am not too sure yet. I assume trying to make everything work will be a challenge, trying to communicate and carry out our experiment properly. I am sure that there will be problems, I expect there to be. We just have to tackle what comes our way," Susan said.

Susan was talking to a Chicago-based reporter, when she saw two little children holding photos of her. They both looked to be about four or five years old.

When she finished talking to the Chicago reporter, she tried to get to the kids to sign their photos.

"Guys right there, those two kids, get them up here so I can sign for them please," Susan said to the mob of reporters.

They all tried to move out of the way as the mother tried to push her two kids to the front.

"Hi guys, what are your names?" Susan asked.

The children were shy, but had the happiest looks on their faces.

"This is Kyle and this is Brittany," the mother said speaking for the stunned kids.

"Here let me sign that for you," Susan said. She realized that neither she nor the kids had a pen or marker. She would need help from the crowd.

"Does anybody have a marker here that I can use?" Susan asked the crowd loudly.

"I have a sharpie," a reporter yelled from the back of the crowd.

"Just send it up here please," Susan said.

She looked up, and saw a marker flying through the sky.

"I like your creativity dude," she said as she quickly tried to catch it. The crowd laughed as she completely missed the marker which flew past her.

"Ok here you go," Susan said to the kids after it was retrieved by another reporter. She signed both of their photos and inscribed *To Kyle and Brittany- Follow your dreams, because they will come true.*

"Thank you so much Dr. King," the mother said. The two kids were still frozen in time because Susan signed for them. They were both looking at the rather unusual signature that Susan had. Her signature looked like a bunch of scribbles with a big chess piece drawn in the middle. This was one of the first autographs she had to sign and it would not be her last.

"Hey Chuck, get these three inside the building, get them seats ... tell security they are my guests," Susan said to the driver.

She continued to do interviews until her thirty minutes was done.

"Sorry guys, I have to get inside now. I will come back later, afterwards," Susan said.

"Thank you," the reporters said. It sounded like a very unorganized chant at a baseball game, all saying the same thing but not synchronized. A blur of similar words.

She walked into the convention hall with her driver. She put her sunglasses on her head.

"Phew! That was exhausting," Susan said. She was exhausted from all of the people and noise, as she had never experienced interviews by the masses.

"I cannot imagine how you put up with that," Chuck said.

"You do not have to imagine," Susan replied comically.

They walked to the lobby where many of the doctors and scientists were waiting and having a small luncheon. The luncheon was for guests only, not members of the public.

Everyone turned as Susan entered the large lobby of the building.

She walked the room and talked with people for about a minute each. Being a large figure, she thought it would make her look good if she greeted people like politicians do.

She honestly did not like talking to all of the people because she wanted to rest before her big speech. And she was claustrophobic, so big events were not her favorite to attend.

She was not paying attention to time; luckily Chuck was.

"Ma'am, we have thirty minutes until your speech," Chuck whispered into Susan's ear.

"Alright."

She finished talking with people at the table she was at and then walked up to the stage.

"Where is my speech?" Susan asked Chuck as they were walking towards the backstage waiting room.

"It will be on the podium and on the two teleprompters," Chuck said.

"Also, there will be press at the back of the room and two projectors on each side of the stage showing your PowerPoint slides," Chuck said.

"Alright thanks. Who made the slides?" Susan asked. She was not aware of a slideshow presentation.

"Most likely Cynthia," Chuck said.

Susan was sitting waiting to go on stage. She could hear the person on stage talking and the crowd applauding. It sounded like a large crowd.

Susan felt anxiety and nervous at the same time, because it was her first huge speech that she needed to get just right. Her problem was she did not write the speech.

It was her time to shine, as she heard the closing remarks of the speaker before her.

"This will truly be a revolutionary study that will change the word science forever. To talk about The Kingston Experiment, I now welcome Dr. Susan Kingston," the speaker said.

Susan walked onto the large stage very confidently. She got to the podium and needed to quickly assess the size and layout of the convention hall.

"Thank you, thank you," Susan said into the microphone. The crowd was so loud, it was almost deafening. Susan noted where her teleprompters were and began her speech. She realized how difficult using the microphone was because the hall was so large and there was a microsecond delay for the sound to be heard through the speakers that caused a slight but annoying echo.

"My name is Susan Kingston. I grew up in Honolulu, Hawaii. When I was in grade school, I read an article about the brain, and I was hooked from that point on. My father, the late Dr. Leon Kingston worked as a clinical researcher. Throughout his many years conducting research, he struck gold when he discovered the cure to Alzheimer's disease. It was a disease that decayed the brain. He was then promoted to the Head of the Center of Disease control and that was when we moved to New York. I graduated college with a PhD in psychology and got the idea for this experiment. At that time my father was still the head of the CDC.

"Over the two years when I was planning my experiment, he became more and more ill. He assigned me to be his successor as the Head. I currently fulfill his duties as the Head. And I followed through with the Kingston Experiment.

"What the Kingston Experiment will test is, how does society affect a regular person? If given the chance to stand up and make a change, will they? That is what I wanted to test. We are going to get the experiment officially started three years from today. We need volunteers who will get a bank account deposit of one million dollars that will gain interest. The hopes of this experiment will be to find out as much about human logic as we can.

"If you want to be a part of this experiment, I will be having a briefing for volunteers in Chicago next month. Contact my office at 800-460-9867 if you are interested to be in my experiment.

"I am confident that this will change the world as we know it... We just need to get the idea spread so everyone knows what this is all about.

"Thank you," Susan concluded. The crowd gave her a standing ovation. Millions of people were watching live on television. And within the first three hours after her speech, ten million people called to possibly be in the experiment. Susan had just finished her first major speech and a feeling of pride overcame her.

The person who introduced her then walked out onto the stage.

"Ladies and gentlemen Dr. Kingston will be answering questions for the next hour," he said. Susan was not expecting this.

Susan answered questions for the entire hour. She was asked everything from what was her favorite color to what her dream vacation would be. She was surprised by the fact that the press was so creative in asking questions. Some of the questions caught her off guard, as she was not expecting them.

After the time was up, Susan was so tired that she wanted to go directly to her car. She did not want to do more interviews. It seemed that her entire day was one giant interview.

Chuck escorted her through the building and outside to the mob of fans. The crowd was chanting, "Susan! Susan! Susan!"

Chapter Thirteen

"Dr. Susan, it's me, Derek."

"I am so sorry, I must have dozed off again daydreaming about how this all started," Susan said.

"It is fine, but I want to show you something," Derek said.

"Alright," Susan said.

Derek escorted Susan to his office where John was watching the live cameras. On one screen the video was paused because it was the one Derek was about to show Susan.

"So, the boy was talking to his sister about her stay at the station. She tells him that she was questioned by monotone voices. He is confused as to why the sister was questioned. He goes to his mom and talks to her, but it is her expressions that are important. Watch and let me know what you think," Derek said.

On the screen, Susan saw the boy and his mother, from the security camera in the kitchen. The mother was at an angle so she had to turn her head to see the camera, as did the boy. The audio was pretty clear, despite the size of the camera.

"Mother, what did my sister do at the Condemning Station?" the boy asked.

"Well honey, I am not sure," the mother stated. She looked worried, which was unusual for her.

"Why did they ask her questions?" the boy asked.

"Oh, why I am unsure," the mother said. She responded quickly to his question, as if she was trying to cover something up.

"They were concerned about her; the occupation ceremony is looming in the near future. They wanted to find her niche in society," the mother said. She sounded nervous and unsure about what she was stating.

The mom then turned and looked directly at the camera in a worried way. The boy then turned around and noticed the small circular camera.

"It ends here. This is what I wanted to show you. Your thoughts?" Derek asked Susan.

"Well I think that the boy is starting to realize something. I think the mother was trying to convey something to us via the stare, but what though?" Susan asked.

"When was this recorded?" Susan asked following up her own question.

"About fifteen minutes ago, but you were sleeping so I didn't wake you right away," Derek said.

"Let's see the live stream," Susan said.

John turned the volume up on the live camera and put it center on the wall as the primary focus.

Chapter Fourteen

I needed to discover more about the questioning from my sister. Mother did not know anything, but she seemed nervous.

I entered my sleeping room where my sister was writing. Writing was a popular time user, and people could convey their thoughts, usually neutral, about things.

"I know you are behind me," she said because she sensed my presence.

"I want to talk to you again," I said.

"Do you ever get that feeling like you are always being watched, or as if a member of society is behind you all the time?" she asked.

"Actually, I do. I do not like the feeling, but it is always there," I said.

"When I was in the Condemning Station, I was in a room that had a door and nothing else but a black chair and white walls. I noticed a tiny black circular object in the intersection of the walls," my sister said.

"I just saw one in the cooking room," I said.

"I was confused, because there were members of society talking asking questions, but I could not see them. I could only hear them," she said.

"What did they request of you?" I asked.

"I recall one female voice asking, 'If you are witnessing a bad thing what do you do?'" my sister said.

"What did you reply?" I asked.

"I said 'It depends on what is happening, but I attempt to intervene'," my sister said.

"I would too... at least I think I would," I said.

"Another question was like 'what would you do if you had total control over someone?' I replied, 'I would not want control, I would act the same with or without control'," my sister said.

"Why would they ask you that? It seems so out-of-the-ordinary," I said.

It was time to go to the EC. When we arrived, everything was just like a regular day.

I went to my classes, at the regular time, obtained new knowledge, and consumed the same food at the regular time.

Every day, I sat next to the same youths during the break when I consumed food. I noticed two youth that were slightly advantaged in height interacting with a younger youth. I had never noticed the three youth interacting before. The two advantaged youth were slowly moving the other youth towards the corner. That was when I recalled the Social Indifference rule. It stated that "Any mistreatment or inequality of one through actions is punishable severely, with a no tolerance standard." I did not know what the punishment was, but I was afraid of what could happen to me if I was caught. I felt sympathetic for the youth being mistreated, because he was vulnerable because self defense was not tolerated.

I was hesitant to act against the mistreatment, but I felt it should've been stopped. I heard the younger child start to cry, which was a very rare emotion in our society. An emotion of outstanding pain.

I then recalled that the Occupation Ceremony was not long away, and if I acted and was reprimanded, my future could be destroyed.

More and more youth started to notice the event. The teachers were watching, but not resolving the situation. They were looking neutrally.

I walked slowly towards the three youth. I was about ten measurements away when I said one word, "Stop!"

The two advantaged youth turned toward me and then continued what they were doing.

I did not know what to do, because I attempted to intervene, without any results. I did not know what would terminate the mistreatment.

I approached the two youth and put my hands on them and pushed them away from the younger youth.

I asked the younger youth a question, "Are you ok?"

"Yes, they alarmed me," the youth said.

That was when the teacher came and took me to the office. She did not look angry or pleased.

"Follow me please," she said to me in a monotone, expressionless voice.

"Ok," I said. I followed her to the office. She had me sit in the solid blue chair.

"Why am I here?" I asked.

"You broke The Code," the teacher said. I was very worried because I broke a rule of The Code. I did not want to be sent to the Condemning Station like my sister.

"I was just trying to help the youth, I felt bad for him," I said.

The teacher looked very confused with what I said. She was confused as to why I felt feelings for another person.

"Your parental unit will be here to remove you," she said.

"Ok," I said. I was worried that I was going to be reprimanded severely.

My mother came from her occupation, to remove me from the situation. She did not look very angry, but she did not look happy. I could tell from her facial expressions that she was not pleased with the situation at hand.

After we got in the rac, my mom started to talk to me.

"Why did you do that?" she asked me.

"I felt bad for the other youth, so I felt I needed to help," I said.

"It is none of your business what is happening to others, only what is happening to you," my mom said.

"I just did not want something bad to happen to the boy," I said. I was scared because I did not know what my mother would do to me as a result of what I did.

"Where are we going?" I asked.

"I am taking you to the Condemning Station, so you will learn a lesson," she said. I did not want to go to the Condemning Station, because I recalled what happened to my sister.

"Ok," I said hopelessly.

It took us an unknown amount of time to get to the Condemning Station. The only difference from last time is that my sister and father weren't with us and that I was the one being condemned.

I saw the same lady at the same desk wearing the same clothing. She took me the same way as she did my sister. She took me to a large white room. There was one black chair in

✕   The King's Pawn

the center of the room and a tiny circular object that was the same one my sister described.

I sat and waited for an unknown amount of time, because there were no time objects in the room. I was startled by a female voice talking to me. It sounded very machine like, but at the same time had enthusiasm. It sounded different than most.

"You can hear me?" the voice asked. The voice was projected quite loudly in the tiny room I was in. I could not determine where the sound was coming from, because the walls were plain.

"Yes, I can hear you," I said. I did not know what else to say or how to reply.

"Good, I am going to ask you questions. You will answer. It's that simple... no tricks," the voice said. I was confused as to which member of society the voice I was hearing belonged to.

"Who are you?" I asked.

"It is entirely irrelevant. Call me ma'am," the voice said.

"Alright, ma'am," I said sarcastically. I knew it was a person I was talking to because the voice wanted to be addressed by the proper title and the voice responded to my questions.

"First question, you cannot get this wrong. Say the first ten numerical values," the voice said.

"One, two, three, four, six, eight, ten, twelve, fourteen and eighteen," I said. I realized that I had made a mistake by saying some values listed as odd, which were not valid in our society.

"Ok great job. Next question, these get harder and harder every time. I want you to tell me the color of the sky during the day," the voice said.

"The sky is blue, not dark or light, but blue," I said truthfully.

"Alright, now where does your mother work?" the voice asked.

"I am unsure as to the location ma'am," I said.

"Okay, next question. Why did you act in the situation today?" the voice asked.

"I was doing what I felt was the right thing. I felt bad for the youth who was being mistreated, so I felt I needed to stop it," I said.

"Was he being bullied?" the voice asked me.

"Mistreated, he was being mistreated. I do not recall the term bullied," I said.

"Bullying is when someone or a group of individuals use their advantage of strength to influence the victim into bad situations. Now tell me based on this, was the youth being bullied?" the voice said.

"I am not sure ... I do know that the youth was being mistreated," I said.

"So, was the youth being bullied?" I asked.

"I cannot confirm or deny any allegations," the voice said.

"Next question, there is an amount of currency on the walkway, what do you do?" the voice asked.

"I give it to the condemning station," I said.

"Are you real?" the voice asked me.

"Are you asking if I am a real member of society?" I replied.

"I am just asking are you real. You tell me," the voice responded.

"I am real, I am talking to you, unless you are unreal," I said. I was slightly confused why this voice was asking me these questions, but I knew there was a reason, but I could not figure out the reason.

"I enjoy your sarcastic remarks, but I do not have time to waste," the voice said as if it was offended.

"Now please prove to me you are real," the voice said.

"I am talking to you right now. If I was not real, you would not be questioning me," I said.

"Ok. Please tell me one proven fact," the voice told me.

"Anything?" I asked.

"Yes," the voice responded.

"E is equivalent to the value of m times the value of c squared," I said. It was a simple math formula I remembered from the Education Center.

"Prove E is equivalent to MC squared," the voice replied.

"Okay. Energy equals the mass times the velocity of light squared," I said confidently.

"You need to prove that it is true," the voice said.

"Well, we obtained the knowledge at the Education Center," I said.

"Very well then... can you disprove this fact?" the voice asked.

"No, because I have been told it is factual, so it must be true," I said.

"Okay. You cannot prove it is real but you cannot prove it is fake either," the voice said.

"Yes ..." I said.

"Interesting. Only a few more questions. What would you do if you were put in a place with violence and absolutely no perfect anything?" the voice asked. It was hard to imagine a place it was describing. Such a place I would not want to see.

"I would not do anything since our society is not the place you are speaking of," I said.

"Ok, where are you right now?" the voice asked.

"I am at the Condemning Station," I replied.

"No really? Where are you?" the voice asked firmly.

"I just told you, I am at the Condemning Station," I said.

"And where is the Condemning Station located?" the voice asked.

"In the universe and in our society," I said.

The member of society who was the voice was angry because she yelled the next line at me.

"Tell me, where are you?"

"I just told you, and it is a sign of respect to listen to the voices of others, which you are not," I said to the rude voice.

I heard a different voice talking to the female voice. She was not talking to me but to another.

"He thinks he knows everything! He doesn't, and he insults me!" the voice said faintly.

"Susan calm down. Do not get angry," a male voice said.

"How can I not get ..." the voice said.

That was when the audio stopped, and the silence returned. I was confused who Susan was, because I never heard the name Susan before. It sounded majestic.

I was in the Condemning Station for three days. It was very boring, and the same voice kept asking me questions. On day four, day four was different from the others.

I woke up to the sound of the voice talking. She was telling me to wake up, and it woke me up.

"On the wall you will see images, tell me your thoughts and ideas about each of them," the voice said.

The first photo was one of a sunrise. The grass was green, the sky blue, the sun yellow, but there was a small structure near the horizon.

"I see a sunrise with a structure. The landscape looks nothing like I have seen before, and the structure looks irregular. It looks like something from a fictional universe," I said.

"Ok, here is the next one," the voice said.

The second picture was of a very large society. There were many large structures, each very unique and a blue body of water, but not just blue, a mixture of blue. At the bottom of the picture spelled out in letters was M-I-A-M-I.

"I see a large society with water, but it looks impure because it is not blue. I see *meame* at the bottom," I said mispronouncing Miami. "The society looks odd to me because each structure is different."

"What is different about this photo?" the voice asked.

"Well for one the hue of the water and the structures are different than here," I said.

"Indeed, they are. This next one is a video," the voice said.

The video started to play. It showed a society that looked very different. The street was broken, the structures unmaintained. I hated looking at the video.

"Please stop this video! I do not like it, it is too much," I said.

"We must go on," the voice said.

"No, we must not," I said.

"This is real, be happy you do not have to live in it like I do," the voice said.

"What do you mean?" I asked.

"I mean nothing," the voice said.

"What do you mean by real, because society does not look like that," I said.

"You will see eventually I guarantee it. Just wait," the voice said.

I was scared because the place I saw on the wall horrified me. I would never want to see a place like that.

My mother came to remove me from the Condemning Station later that day. I was very happy she did. I did not want to stay any longer or see any more pictures. I still had that horrific video stuck in my head, it horrified me.

"Mother is there a place where things are broken?" I asked my mother as we were returning to our LOO.

"Yes, NO ... no, there is not," she replied. She said yes and immediately changed her response to no.

"Who is Susan?" I asked.

"She is my, she is most likely a member of society who works to assist members in need," my mom said.

I noticed that my mom recognized the name instantly, based on how quickly she responded.

"The Occupation Ceremony is soon, what are you interested in doing?" my mother asked me.

"I want to work somewhere of interesting status, I want to find Susan," I said.

"You will not find Susan, what do you want to do for your adult life?" she asked me.

"I want to question people and confuse them like Susan did to me," I said.

I did not realize how much the interrogation changed my mental status, I came out with a completely different goal in adult life.

"You can be the secretary at the Condemning Station, because there is no occupation to confuse people," my mother said.

"Well, I hope that the elders choose the right occupation for me," I said.

"Me too, honey, I hope so too," my mother said to me.

Chapter Fifteen

The Occupation Ceremony was one fifty-secondth of a full cycle away. During education, we started to act the ceremony out. The educators took us to the Community Hall, which was next to our Education Center. All of the youth sat in the seats of the structure that was called the Theater by the educators.

"So, on the morning of the ceremony, you are to sit by our order on stage. Each row will be called up at a time to line up. You will stand on the left in relation to the audience. One per time you will walk to the Chief Elder who will assign you to your occupation. You will then return to your seat without talking until the ceremony concludes," the educator said.

The chairs were set up for the ceremony, so the educators assigned us to a seat. My sister sat to my right and another youth to my left. I did not talk to him because it was against The Code.

It was the morning of the ceremony.

I woke up at exactly six in the morning. I was very excited because I would find out what my occupation would be for the rest of my life. I took a shower and went to consume food. My sister was already eating food that my dad had made for her. My mom was also eating food, the same as my sister.

"Good morning," I said.

"Hi, how are you son?" my dad asked.

"I am excited for the ceremony," I said.

"Me too, I am a little scared also," my sister said.

"You should not be scared honey, we all went through the same ceremony and got our occupations. You should just enjoy the moment," my mother said.

"It will be hard, but I will try to enjoy the moment," I said.

"I went through the same ceremony. I was in your place at one time," my mom said. The way she said it was different as if she wanted to try to make us feel better.

My mother had chosen a different outfit for me to wear, one with a jacket and pants, and a tie, it was known as a suit. She also chose a red dress for my sister to wear.

After we consumed our food and got ready, we left for the ceremony. My sister and I talked during the trip to the theater.

"What occupation do you think I will get?" she asked me.

"I am not sure. You are very patient, so possibly a medical occupation," I said.

"I hope not, I cannot stand the sight of blood," she said.

"Then you will not make a good doctor or parent," I said.

"Behave and be nice to each other. Just act normal please do it for me, I do not want to be embarrassed by my youth," my mother said.

"Maybe an energy producer," I whispered to my sister. Everyone in society knew that working to make energy was very difficult. It was safe, but long hours, an occupation that was very undesirable.

We arrived exactly one hour early. Some other youth and their guardians had arrived, but not too many. My sister and I wanted to get to our seats to just relax.

"Mom, can we go to our seats?" she asked.

"No," my dad said.

"Why not?" my sister asked.

"Because it is too early," dad replied.

"Go in," my mom said.

"We will see you inside," I said to my parents.

My sister and I went directly to our seats. We did not talk, but just stared at the immaculate structure we were in. It was very unproportional. The ceiling was arched, the seats were not in line with each other. There were drawings on the glass that did not have right angle intersections. The color was not a solid white, but rather a mixture of white and yellow.

As members of society arrived, the structure became more crowded, but still very silent, because nobody talked. The last youth to arrive did so sixteen minutes before eleven, when the ceremony was to begin.

11:00 am

The Chief Elder was sitting in his place and all of the youth were silent.

The theater was fully occupied with members of society. I was very nervous because I was going to discover my lifetime occupation.

One of the educators stood up and spoke to the attendees. She just spoke at regular conversation tone.

"Members of society, you are here to witness a major step in the life of a youth. It is the step from being a youth to being a member of society, an adult. Each youth will be assigned an occupation from the Chief Elder. We shall begin now," the educator said.

I saw a woman rush in from the left side of the theater. She looked different from every other member of society.

Susan King was a person who hated being late to events. At ten o'clock the morning of the Occupation Ceremony, Susan realized that she wanted to see the experiment in person. She had recently interrogated the boy, but she wanted to see what the experiment really looked like. The last time Susan had been inside the society was to get a tour when it was finished some fifteen years earlier.

She drove a black SUV into the experiment from the headquarters. She had to try to blend in with the very unrealistic environment of the King's Pawn.

She had to find a way to get to the theater by eleven exactly, because she did not want to be late. She faced a slight delay in timing when she reached the one and only entrance point to the society.

The guard who was to keep the huge gate closed at all times was surprised when he saw a black SUV speeding towards him.

He walked in front of the gate putting his body between the speeding SUV and the gate. As expected, the black car stopped before him.

"Hello ma'am, how may I be of assistance," he said.

"Let me in that's how," Susan said.

"Sorry I am not allowed to permit any entry to this property under the government of United Kingdom," the guard said.

"Well I have a speech here in ten minutes," Susan said.

"What is your name," he asked.

"Susan King," Susan said.

"That is what they all say ... well, there are not any 'theys' because 'they' don't ever reach me," the guard said. Susan realized that the guards said the same thing the last time she tried to get on the property.

"Well I am the head of this experiment and I am requesting access," Susan said.

"Access denied, please reroute to highway 75 about forty miles that way," the guard said.

"Do you know how many crazies try to get in here... a lot, so get back to the crazy lady's highway ... it is back that way lady!" he continued.

Susan kept a pepper spray can and a tranquilizer in her car just in case she needed a non-lethal attack. She also had a 22-millimeter handgun, for emergencies, as she was the head of the most important experiment to ever be done.

"Alright then. Hey, can I see your identification badge, mister?" Susan asked.

As the guard went into his small hut to get his badge, Susan shot him with a tranquilizer that could keep a bear out for two hours.

"You won't mind that I hope," Susan said.

"Well I guess I just joined the club ... and it feels great!" Susan said.

Susan still could not get the gate open, not even the guard could. He was just there as a precaution. Susan would need help.

She picked up her phone.

"Hey Commander, go to my computer," Susan said. She had called the Commander who answered immediately, as all hands were on deck for the Occupation Ceremony.

"Why? Where are you? We have been trying to find you," Commander asked.

"Sitting at the entrance to society, next to a guard who may or may not have been tranquilized by me," Susan said.

"Ok, ok. Why are you going into the experiment?" Commander asked.

"Just let me in please I'll talk as I drive to the theater," Susan said.

"Alright, I'm at your computer," Commander said. He was a bit confused that Susan was trying to get into the experiment. Given the fact that Susan was the boss, he did not want to question her.

"Ok, now go to the security access, and select main gate and then hit the enter key, it will ask for a password. The password is 12345678," Susan said.

"It's not working," Commander said.

"Idiot it's 2444666668888888. Did you really think I had no reasoning between the easiest password ever?" Susan said.

"Yes, maybe I did," Commander said.

"Well if it fooled you then it can fool anyone," Susan said as she laughed.

"How could that man fall for the 1234 trick," Susan muttered to herself.

The gate opened, and Susan entered and waited for it to close behind her.

She talked with the Commander while driving to the theater. She knew the layout of the society and knew she really, really had to rush. The drive would take about thirty minutes when she had less than half of that.

"Commander I want to see what this experiment is really like, what do these people actually live like?" Susan said.

"They live," Commander said, being interrupted by Susan.

"It's not a question it's a statement," Susan said.

"By the way get through to security that I am myself and to let me in when I tell them! It's so annoying what I have to put up with, when I can easily fire them on spot," Susan said.

"Oh, and also what is with the attitude! The crazy lady's expressway is that way... give me a break already!" Susan said angrily.

"Well that is just terrible," Commander said.

"Tell me about it!" Susan said.

"Yes, ma'am I will have every member of the team addressed about that," Commander said. He would follow through with his promise.

He knew that this was the proper time to question Susan.

"Why exactly did you want to go inside the experiment?" Commander asked.

"I want to see what I did and also keep tabs on my experiment, the only way I can do that is in person," Susan said.

"I get it, but you have to be extremely careful not to mess anything up, the littlest mistake by you will cause an immediate contamination of results. You have to remember everything works like the finest clock known to man!" Commander said.

"I will be very careful, that's why I took your SUV, it drives very nicely. They did a good job making that tank move quickly," Susan said.

"I love my car, but I want it back in one piece because you took my actual personal car not the government one!" Commander said strictly. He knew that Susan was not the best driver.

"Yep! Just know that it is under the name of science, this car will work fine. Plus, it is solid black, nobody will question it," Susan said confidently.

As she began to drive through the society, she was noticing how perfect everything was. The colors, the shapes, everything was perfect.

"How did we manage to do this?" Susan asked. She was referring to the perfection of the details that she wanted to use in the test.

"You came up with all of the ideas, you even drew the preliminary drawings of the houses," Commander said.

"I truly never realized how perfect this world is," Susan said. "The tediousness and attention to detail is amazing!"

She was driving down Main Street, where the Condemning Station was located. She did not like the appearance of the Condemning Station, because she was not the person to design the physical appearance.

"This police station looks so much better through cameras," Susan said.

"Well it is one of the few buildings you did not create ma'am," Commander said.

"Yes, the only other building I did not have a part in creating was the theater, but I think it turned out fine based on the cameras. I'm about to see it in person, my opinion on the theater may change," Susan said.

She was very worried that she was drawing too much attention to herself by driving through the society in a vehicle that did not match any in the experiment. People were looking at the car, but they were not really evaluating the situation for what it really was.

"It's this car I am worried most about," Susan said.

The vehicles for the King's Pawn were not like any others. They were all hand-picked and simplified and modified. For example, the car of the mother, the white sedan was not just a sedan. Susan liked the futuristic look that cars in movies had. She needed a cheap car that would be easy to modify.

The Ford Fusion was affordable and powerful. Susan met with the owner of the Ford Motor Company, and bought a large quantity of cars for a reduced price. Susan's money coordinator was the person who actually paid Ford the 3 million dollars for the cars. Many different mod shops agreed to modify the cars to the liking of Susan King. They would get credit in the end because they were able to put commercials on television. For the more unique vehicles, the process was different.

There were many vehicles unique to the King's Pawn that the outside world had never seen.

The bus that took the kids to the school was entirely custom made. The bus was a regular school bus that the accountant bought from a school bus company in Tennessee. A mod shop in California did the unique vehicles. They rebuilt the body of the bus to be square in shape. The interior was redone to the needed perfection of the experiment. A lot more minor work was done to it, but it had no major effect in the long run.

The most tedious concept of the experiment was the perfect measurements. Throughout the process fifteen contractors were on hand to measure every single thing to be an even number. Susan was not joking when she said she wanted everything to be even in measurement, as the contractors would find out.

Luckily, Susan was not noticed by many members of society, because they learned that everything was the same every day, so little details went unnoticed ... even huge ones.

The one thing Susan did like was the colors of society. They were all perfect, engineered to look solid. The only color that was not actually a perfect color was the blue of the sky. The pawns did not realize that the sky was not actually the solid blue, but rather a lighter blue. Over the years, their brains told their eyes that it was the same as every other blue, when in reality it was different.

"This place looks so amazing, the colors are so stunning," Susan said.

"Yes, they are, I agree," Commander said.

"I would love to live in a place with these colors," Susan rambled.

"You do, you had your office and house made with the same design of colors," Commander said.

"Oh yeah you are right ... Well this is just amazing," Susan said.

Susan went on a slight detour to drive past the home of the pawns. She knew which block they lived on due to the semi-hidden cameras. The members of society learned to ignore the cameras as they did the real color of the sky.

"Wow, we should make a museum out of this block after this is done," Susan said. She actually would consider the idea of a museum, but while driving carefully was not the right time.

"So, what exactly do you plan to say?" Commander asked.

"Well I have a paper from my desk that I wrote simple notes on, but I can just improvise most of it," Susan said.

"Wait! Which paper?" Commander asked.

"My personal ones with the, the experiment name on it," Susan said stuttering because of distractions as she drove.

"You cannot use that, if they see that, this is all doomed," Commander said.

"That is why I told you not to go inside, because there are too many risks involved," Commander said.

"I will just be very, very careful," Susan said.

"No! Do not do it," Commander said.

"Well I could have told you that ... it is too late now! I am here," Susan said. This was a tense realization, as it hit Susan that she could really ruin her experiment with one mistake.

Susan was nearing the theater, she could see the cars parked outside.

"Where shall I park the tank?" Susan asked.

"Well looking at the cameras, I can see you coming. Park near the exit of the building, but do not block it," Commander said.

"Alright I will do that," Susan said.

Susan parked the Commanders SUV near the exit of the theater, but out of view from anyone who is inside the theater.

She entered the theater and was stunned by what she saw. All of the eyes silently turned to her, the way a hawk eyes its prey. She was stunned how silent they were, a pin could be heard literally. She saw the two pawns immediately, and she noticed that they saw her. Internally, Susan was creeped out by all of the silent ghost like figures, she just was not expecting the silence.

The woman had hair of a mixed color. It was not just brown, but had another color mixed in.

She walked with a flawed gait towards the podium that was solid brown. She had a paper in her hand, that had her topic of speech on it.

When she started talking, I noticed that her voice sounded very real. She had emotion in each word she said, unlike most members of society. She also spoke at an uneven pace, which I actually liked the sound of.

"Hello everyone, my name is Susan Kingston. I am here today to congratulate each and every one of your children, youth, my bad. Over the last fifteen years you have shown the ability to function not as youth but as grown adults. You have worked hard to get to where you are now and will continue to work to contribute to society. I wish you and your parents, I mean guardians the best of luck over the following years, and I hope you learn to love your new job, I mean occupation," Susan said. She expected a loud applause but was surprised by a perfectly timed rhythmic clapping pattern.

Susan, I recognized the name, it was the same name as the member of society who questioned me. Could this be the same lady?

The Chief Elder stood up and walked to the podium where he spoke to Susan. I could not hear what he said to her, because the distance sound traveled was not great enough to reach our location.

"You will now stand up as a row and proceed to me as I point at you," the Chief Elder said.

I was in the second row, so our turn to get our occupation was very close. I was very anxious to find out what I would be. I hoped I would be given an interesting occupation. Knowing that there was a possibility of receiving a bad occupation added to the nerves. I saw Susan greeting the youth after they were told what their occupation was.

I was worried based on the first few occupations, Energy Producer, Educator, Education Bus Transporter. The only favorable occupation was Knowledgments Assistant. They were responsible for creating books made by the Knowledgments who found the information to be put in the books.

Before I knew it, my row was up.

I was very nervous, between the gathering of society members, the Chief Elder, and my future. I was the fourth person in the row. My sister was third.

The first occupation was Driver, a very interesting occupation. The second of the row was a medical assistant.

The Chief Elder pointed at my sister, and she began the slow walk towards the center of the stage.

"You will be ... a Deathmaster," the Chief Elder said. My sister walked past Susan and back to her seat. I was surprised my sister was given the occupation of Deathmaster, I knew she would not agree with the decision.

I was next. I was very nervous, as I would be given my life occupation. I hoped to receive an occupation that would allow me to live in a bigger LOO. There were only a few occupations that gave large LOO's, so I knew that the probability of me being assigned one was very low.

The Chief Elder pointed at me, so I began the slow walk to him. It seemed like I was walking forever, when in reality it was only about a few seconds. The audience seemed frozen, and they were silent. I saw them out of the corner of my eyes because I was focused on the Chief Elder and Susan with tunnel vision.

When I reached the Chief Elder, he said only one word to me.

"Hi."

He then reached into the podium where a cylindrical object was. It was a piece of paper that was rolled up.

"This youth has been assigned a very special occupation. He is to report to the Hall of Society the succeeding day," the Chief Elder said addressing the audience.

I noticed that Susan had a very pleased facial expression after the Chief Elder addressed me, but I did not know why.

I walked over to her because I had to talk to her. I knew that was my only chance to ever speak to her, so I decided to approach her.

"I know who you are, Susan," I said. She had an obvious change of physical emotion like the news surprised her.

"Ok," she said confused.

I walked back to my seat and waited for the ceremony to end. But I had curiosity as to what I was handed.

I unrolled the paper and it read in type lettering.

You have a Special Role in Society.

You have one of the most important roles. You will find out your occupation by reporting to the Hall of Society the day following that of the Occupation Ceremony.

You will be addressed once again by the Chief Elder at eight before noon.

I sat for the rest of the ceremony and watched as each youth was given an occupation. I was excited to find out what my occupation was.

After the ceremony concluded, I wanted to talk to my sister, but I had to wait until we returned to our LOO.

We were walking to the rac, when I noticed a large rac that was black in color. Also, it did not look normal, the shape and contour was unlike any other rac. It was in the wrong location, but I did not know why.

"Mother, why is that rac located near the exit?" I asked as I pointed to the black rac.

"I am unsure," my mom replied.

"Who is in possession of it?" I asked.

"Again, I do not know," my mom said.

As we were driving away, I saw a female figure, that of Susan walk to the rac.

"Mom, that is the rac of Susan," I said. I was curious as to why Susan not only looked different than members of society, but also drove a different rac and had a different voice.

She did not respond, but I saw that her facial emotion changed.

"So honey, do you like your occupation?" mother asked to my sister trying to change the conversation unnaturally.

"Not really, I did not want to deal with the post death," my sister said.

"I feel sorry for you, because that is a very creepy occupation," I said.

"You should! You know I cannot bare the sight of blood," she said.

"I would not mind the blood, I would be disturbed by the actual remains! I think that aspect is unsettling," I said.

"No, it is an important one, as we will all face an unhappy demise in the end," my mother said.

"Son, what is your occupation?" dad asked.

"I do not know. I have to go to the Hall of Society at eight before noon tomorrow to be told," I said.

"Okay! I think you are going to be a special member as an adult," mom said.

"Maybe ... I was the only member to receive a special occupation. It would be cool to stand out," I said. I wanted to find out more about my sister's occupation.

"What time does your occupation begin?" I asked her.

"At eleven, at the Deathmasters structure," she replied.

"And where is that located?" I asked.

My mother knew the answer, so she answered. "It is near the Emergency Facility."

"Oh, okay," my sister said. "I am a bit unsettled that I have to do this occupation. I did not want to deal with blood or remains. I wanted to do something more interesting."

"Honey, each occupation is unique and interesting in a special way. As time progresses, you will enjoy your occupation," my mom replied.

"That is true. I did not get the best, but he did," my sister said.

I agreed with her statement, in that I likely would end up with a more interesting occupation.

I had yet another important day ahead of me.

Chapter Sixteen

The alarm rang every two seconds starting at 6:00 A.M for two minutes exactly.

It was yet another bright beautiful day. I woke up at 6 exactly, because I wanted to be early, not late. It would be terrible to be late on the first day of a new occupation.

The morning was exactly the same as that of every other, with one new difference, I had an occupation. My sister and father had not yet woken, but my mother was already dressed when I awoke.

After I took my five-minute shower, I went to the cooking room to consume my daily food. My mother was already awake and sitting at the table reading a book.

"Are you excited for your first day of your occupation?" She asked me when she saw me.

"I am worried, because I do not know what I have been assigned," I said.

"You have no need to worry, because each role is vitally important to our society," she said. I was hoping she was right.

"So, what is your role in society?" I asked.

"I cannot tell you, because it is not something you need to know right at this time," she said. Her response seemed suspicious, because there was no obvious reason why I should not know her occupation.

It was seven exactly when my mother and I left to go to the Hall of Society. It was located near the Hall of Knowledge, which was actually not too far from our LOO.

We arrived very early, at half past seven. I decided to enter and find my new occupation by talking to the Chief Elder.

Before I entered, I wanted to say one more thing to my mother.

"I love you mother," I said. I realized I had an odd love for my mother, sister, and father, but I never had the opportunity to voice my feelings.

"I ... I love you too," she said. She was not expecting my expression of emotion.

The Hall of Society was where the Board of Elders met to discuss new ideas. There was a member of society who was at a symmetrical desk.

"Hello, I am here to speak to the Chief Elder," I said.

"Are you here to find your occupation?" she asked me with little emotion.

"Yes," I replied.

"Please follow me," she said. She stood up and walked down a long hallway. There was a door that had a sign next to it "Chief Elder". She knocked on the door two times and then opened it.

"Alright here is the Chief Elder," she said.

"Thank you," I said.

She had already turned around and walked down the hallway.

"Hello?" I said.

"Yes, I am here," an old voice said.

The room I was in was filled with books and papers. They had all sorts of symbols and numbers on them, formulas.

"Are you here to discover your occupation?" he asked. I still could not find him. All I found was a very large wall with thousands of books. His room was very large and it was made up of various rooms.

"Yes," I said.

"Hi, I am the Chief Elder," he said. He came through a doorway. His white hair was neatly combed and he was wearing a red shirt and black pants.

"Hello sir," I said. He looked much more aged than he did at the ceremony.

"Here is the paper," I said as I handed him the paper.

"No need to give it to me," he said as he returned the paper to me.

"Ah yes, so for your occupation, you will be replacing me," he said.

"You are truthful in your words?" I asked. I did not know what he meant by 'replacing'. The Chief Elder has been the same member for as long as I have been living.

"Very truthful," he replied.

"So, what is my occupation?" I asked.

"You are the new Chief Elder, I am getting very old and am nearing my end, so I needed a replacement," he said.

"I am much too young to be an elder," I said.

"Perhaps you are young, but I will teach you how to rule over society. You will sleep here with me, because you will soon live at my LOO. You will eventually take possession of it after my passing," he said.

"But what about my family?" I asked.

"For the first one-fifty second of the revolution, you will remain at your LOO. Is that acceptable?" he asked.

"Yes sir it is," I said. I was happy I would be able to return home for a while with my family. I was also slightly overwhelmed by the occupation I was given, it was so important.

"Follow me," he said.

He showed me around his workplace. It was bigger than my LOO. It had a cooking room, a computer, and a piano. I was surprised to see a piano, as I had never seen one before. I had only heard them in education and I loved the sound they produced. It was so filling and bold, but it was also very flawed which just added to the glory.

"Sir, do you play the piano?" I asked.

"I do, a little, but I have not played in years," he said.

"Could you play something for me please?" I asked.

"I can attempt," he said. "Keep in mind, I am very old, and not as versatile as I used to be."

He went over to the piano and started to play one of the most beautiful sounds I had ever heard. It was such a rare item in our society due to the imperfect sound it made. I thought the sound was perfect.

"It is so beautiful," I said.

"It has its flaws," he said.

"I think it is perfection," I said.

"Thank you," he said.

"Now we shall talk about what my occupation really is," he said, as he slowly moved to another seat.

"Alright," I said. We sat at a very nice table to talk. I watched as the racs passed by the large circular window.

"So being the Chief Elder is a huge responsibility. I have complete control of this society and everything goes through me. If we need to amend The Code, I have to approve. If we make new regulations, I have to approve. 'We' is referring to the Board of Elders, which I am the head of also. I have made some of the most important rules to society, such as the education standards," he said.

"So how do you make a new rule?" I asked.

"I write it down and it is immediately added to The Code; the Board of Elders also write possible rules down, that I either accept or deny," he said. "I think about rules for a great deal of time before I ever think about adding them."

"Alright, when would I need to start making new rules?" I asked.

"As soon as you want, you and I are a pair, so the rule has to pass by both of us, and after my passing, you will replace me, and you will be able to make any laws. For now, if you have an idea, I will oversee the addition or rejection of it," he said.

"That is a lot of responsibility," I said.

"Yes it is," the Chief Elder said.

"So I have a question, why did I get chosen? There were so many other youth that could have filled this role" I asked.

"I needed someone with responsibility and I have been watching you over the years. Last week when you prevented that situation at the Education Center. That was when I really made my decision because the Chief Elder needs to be someone who is not afraid to prevent things. Not many members are willing to take actions like you have," he said. I thought about the incident for a second. I was imagining how my life outcome would have been different if I did not act during that one situation.

"We have a lot of paperwork to do because we have to give the exact written wording to be added to The Code," he said.

"What is The Code? Is it a literal document?" I asked.

"You have many questions as a young one typically has, I will answer your questions as the time comes," he said.

"Alright," I said.

We spoke for a few minutes to get to know each other. I did notice that he, like the rest of society, was rather neutral with emotions.

"Since it is early, we still have plenty of time today. Typically I work until two in the afternoon, but there are exceptions," he said.

"What will we be doing?" I asked.

"Well I have to test your ability to solve problems and solve conflict," he said.

"How do you do that?" I asked.

"Well I have this device that wears like that of glasses. It projects a visual to your peripheral vision and central vision along with sounds. You act as if you are in the place of what you are experiencing," he said. He went to get the glasses. When he came back into the room, he was carrying them. They were large in size with ear covers that sound is heard through.

"I have created a variety of situations that you will act in over time, but the first one is very easy to show you what it will be like," he said.

"Interesting," I said.

"Put this on, and then I will direct you from there," he said.

I put on the glasses and I was in another world. I was in an education room where an educator was sitting at his desk. I was the only youth in the room. I looked around and I saw different parts of the room. This device was so realistic it was hard to distinguish between the two.

"Alright, when I say start, the scenario will play out. Just walk to move closer and use these two sensors as your hands," he said as he handed me two cylindrical objects.

"You are just going to act like you would, the only difference is that the situation is not actually happening," he continued.

He began the test. I saw a male educator and an education room with a writing wall behind him.

"Hello," the male educator said.

"Hi," I said.

"Please approach the writing wall," the educator said.

I walked towards the wall as instructed. It was a weird feeling walking to something that was not actually there.

"On this wall I want you to write the Theory of Evolution by Natural Selection as quickly as you can," the educator said.

I wrote as quickly as I could. It was a topic that I had read a lot about because I was interested in science.

> *The Theory of Natural Selection is the theory that nature will choose the best traits needed and the other ones will be adapted. Thus species evolve to adapt to their environment. For example when...*

"Please stop," the educator said.

I stopped mid statement.

"Fantastic," he said.

"Now I want you to, state orally, how to find the slope intercept of a line," the educator said.

"You use two given points to solve the value of y one minus y two divided by the value of x one minus the value of x two," I said. I was taught about formulas in education.

"This next one is not as easy, but if you get it right you can return to your LOO early," the educator said.

"Okay, what is the question?" I asked.

"What are the first one hundred digits of the numerical equation known as Pi?" the educator asked.

I was unsure about the first one hundred digits, but I knew the first few.

"Sir, all I have obtained is 3.141592653," I said.

"That is okay, because today is the first of your many days, you will be released early," the educator said.

The image turned to blackness and I took off the glasses and found myself in a blank room. It had a door, and I saw that I had drew on the walls with a real marker. That was when the Chief Elder entered through the same door.

"This is the Visual Room as I have assigned it. This is where you will be doing the test with the virtual glasses, because this room is designed to be safe and easily damaged and manipulated by you, as you will soon discover," he said.

"Alright," I said. I was a bit unsure what he meant by a destructible room.

"So, it is one hour past midday, and you can return to your LOO as promised. Your guardians will be at their occupation so I can return you," he said.

"Thank you," I said.

I followed the Chief Elder to his rac. It was larger than the one my family had, and it was faster too. I sat in the back of the rac. When the Chief Elder started the rac, I noticed that a small screen turned on and I saw a map that moved as we did.

"What is that screen?" I asked as I pointed to the miniature screen.

"It is a map that allows me to see my location in society, as my memory is not very good anymore, I can, and do easily get lost," he said.

"Very interesting," I said. I did not know that there was such a thing as an interactive map.

"Oh, and another thing, I will be giving you a rac that you will drive to my residence every day. I will teach you how to drive over the next week, but it is my gift to you," he said.

I was not expecting to be rewarded so quickly. I was also scared to drive because I did not know how.

"Wow what an honor, I cannot thank you enough," I said.

We were driving down my street when I noticed that my family was still at their occupations.

Chapter Seventeen

I was chosen to be the Deathmaster's assistant. The Deathmaster dealt with the members of society who lost their life due to age. It was an occupation that not many people wanted, and I was one of those people. It was common for people to be sickened by the sight of blood.

I had to report to the Hall of Death, where one's family could visit the dead relative. I had to learn how to properly do the procedures of the Deathmaster.

I reported to my new occupation at the time I was told the previous day. My brother got a very prestigious occupation, becoming the Chief Elder. I was surprised that I got a very unprestigious occupation. My occupation would allow me to explore new regions of the society because we would take the remains out of the society for burial, so that was what I was looking forward to the most. I wanted to see what has yet to be seen by the majority of others.

I arrived at the location and I knocked on the front door because it was locked. A young secretary answered the door and opened it for me, because the Hall of Death had not opened yet. She must have been expecting me because she came to the door quickly.

"Hello," I said to the member of society.

"Hi," she replied.

"I am here as the Deathmasters assistant," I said. The lady looked unfazed, as most members of society did.

"Alright please wait in the room of waiting," she said neutrally.

I sat down and waited patiently, I was always more patient than my brother. He did not like to wait for things, but I did not mind to. I quickly noticed how comforting the chairs in the waiting room were, so that made the process less undesirable.

About ten minutes later, I was greeted by the Deathmaster. He was about forty years of age, and was dressed in a suit, much like the one my brother wore to the occupation ceremony. The Deathmaster was very well kept in his posture, as he walked with purpose and every motion was methodically thought out.

"You are the Assistant to the Deathmaster?" he asked.

"Yes, I am," I said happily. I wanted to look like I cared about my new occupation because first looks are how one makes first impressions.

"Alright, let us get started," he said.

We walked into an office that had a solid brown desk and two black chairs. It was very basic and simplistic. The Deathmaster sat behind the desk on a third black chair.

"So, I will have to show you how I prepare the dead, it is easy once you know how. Here is a book on the simplified process, one that will soon be second nature to you," he said.

I did not think that in reading a book, I would learn the processes. I was always more of a visual learner, I learned new things by doing them repeatedly.

"So how will I become well practiced?" I asked.

"When we are sent a dead member of society, I will do the process and you will watch, and then the second time we will both do the process together, and the third time I will watch as you do the process by yourself," he said.

"That sounds fun," I said. He did not catch my sarcasm when I said fun.

I picked up the book the Deathmaster handed me. It depicted the process of preparing a body, one that looked very unpleasant. I would have to get used to my rather unusual occupation as I would have it for my life and I would likely have to teach a future Deathmaster.

"You can study the book for the following day, as we do not have a dead member of society," the Deathmaster said. "Do you have any questions?"

"Actually, I do," I said. I was thinking of various questions to indirectly obtain knowledge on my new occupation.

"What was the oddest case you have had?" I asked.

"I do not classify any member of society as odd, but unique. Every single member of society is unique. I have had many members of society who have died. Some did not look like they were from our society, but rather from a neighboring society, that was the only out of tune task," the Deathmaster said.

"How do you know where they are from?" I asked.

"Based on physical appearance. To set an example, members from our society have solid colored hair, never a mix. Other societies have a mixture in coloration. That is the main reference, since altering the color of one's natural hair is not allowed due to The Code," the Deathmaster said. I did not really comprehend the idea that there were other people out there, I grew up always thinking we were the only ones.

"Do you like being the Deathmaster?" I asked.

"I am neutral, I was assigned this position, so it was not what I wanted to do. I have accepted my role and I carry out what I have been assigned," he said.

"How about you, are you content being the Deathmaster?" he asked me.

"To be honest, I did not want to deal with the dead, but I have never done it, so I am not sure what to expect," I said.

"To be truthful, it is very difficult the first few times, because this occupation can cause side effects that you may soon experience. You may be emotionally challenged, but you will get over it. I just want you to know that you will change emotionally as a member," he said.

I did not really understand what he meant, but I would figure it out eventually.

"I am sure I will. How do you deal with the members related to the dead?" I asked.

"It is fairly routine, as many people are very neutral, but some do show some emotion, but not a lot. I will show you how, but first let us get started on the very basic concepts," he said.

"Alright," I said, still not knowing what to expect.

My expectations and reality were two different things, as I would soon find out.

Chapter Eighteen

Susan arrived back at the headquarters a short time after she left from the theater. In her mind, her speech went horribly wrong, but to the children in the theater, it went just fine.

Susan, driving the Commanders SUV, sped back through the desert to the headquarters. She parked badly, because she was not a good driver. She did not drive too much as she was always driven. She lost the ability over time. She accidently hit another car parked in the parking lot. She was known for damaging cars and not paying to get them fixed, so she left another note on the car she hit, in attempt to apologize.

She went inside to talk with the Commander and the other workers who were monitoring the cameras and data.

"Hello Commander. Did you like my speech?" Susan asked.

"It was just the loveliest speech ever," Commander said sarcastically.

"It was just shy of the best speech ever spoken," someone else said sarcastically.

"What was so bad about it?" Susan asked. She picked up on the obvious sarcasm her employees were showing her.

"Everything," everyone who was in the room replied almost at the same time.

"Susan, you nearly ruined the experiment ... Again!" Commander said loudly.

"Well ... I did not ruin it, so this visit was fine," Susan said.

"You do not realize what you are risking by going into the experiment... it just is not clicking with you! It will when you make a mistake, but until then you are oblivious!" Commander said.

"It really is fine, nothing will happen," Susan said.

"You say the same thing every single time," Commander said.

"I do not," Susan said.

"Trust me, you do Susan," Commander said. The other workers agreed with the Commander, Susan always used the same excuse.

"Oh yeah I just remembered, how is tomorrow going to work?" Susan asked. She changed the topic of the conversation.

"You planned this, but I will tell you anyways. The boy will be the Chief Elder, and his sister the Deathmaster," Commander said.

"Where will we get the bodies for the Deathmaster?" Susan asked.

"Well we can start a campaign or something," Commander suggested.

"That is an idea," Susan said.

Susan walked over to the drawing wall and started writing. She wrote at the top "Deathmaster."

"So, we will need a way to get bodies," Susan said.

"We can ask for donations," someone said.

"That may not work, and it would not be easy to get people to donate a loved one's remains just because," Susan said.

"Start killing people off," someone said jokingly. The remark caused subtle laughter in the room.

"Definitely will not cause any problems having people killed," Susan said comically and sarcastically.

"Susan, you can offer them money and possibly go meet them in person," Derek said.

"I love that idea," Susan said. "It is always better to have a representative show up to comfort and persuade the family."

"Susan you heard the part about you going to visit the families, right?" Commander asked stressing the word 'you'.

"Yes, I heard it loud and clear. I will get a free reason to travel," Susan said.

What many people did not know about Susan was the fact that she was very immature at times. She would get things done, but she also acted like a child when she got too excited about something. She did well keeping that fact hidden from most, but everyone who worked with her knew about it. She just did not pay attention or show enough care towards her experiment as she needed to, and a careless manager never works out well.

"We need to be careful as we may be a large target for scammers," Commander said.

"Yes indeed," Susan said. She liked to acknowledge people's ideas in a way that it seemed like she had a similar idea, when in reality, she didn't even think of a remote similarity.

The Commander was right, the King's Pawn Experiment was running on very low funds. One of the main sponsors stopped giving his money, because he lost most of it in the stock market. He made a big mistake by investing in only one stock. The budget for the experiment was only eight million dollars per month for Susan King, and if she spent a dime more, she would be in debt. With her uncontrolled spending patterns, the experiment was bound for major debt. It was a matter of days before the seemingly bottomless money well would be used up.

"How much would we offer?" Commander asked.

"May I intervene?" a woman in Headquarters asked. This woman was the assistant to the accountant for the project. When it came to money, she knew the best way to save while still getting the most out of what was spent.

"Statistically speaking, we have no spending money. Our main sponsor stopped sponsoring us due to a lack of money. If we give out any money we would be in debt and the government from every country imaginable would be after us. So, the most we can offer is one hundred and fifteen thousand dollars exactly per family," she said.

"Nobody would donate their loved one for less than a million dollars," Susan said angrily.

"I agree," Commander said.

"A lot of people who do not have money would gladly accept the money. For them it's either bury or cremate their loved one, and fund the burial, or receive thousands, and not have to fund a ceremony," the assistant said.

"That is spot on," Derek yelled from his shared office.

"True, but we need a way to get the message to these people. Does anyone have any ideas as a way to get donators?" Susan asked.

"I think I have an easy idea," John said.

"And your idea is what?" Susan asked.

"The last time you publicized to get people to donate their lives for our experiment, when we were getting on our feet, it worked phenomenally. I say you spend some money on a small tour talking about what has happened so far and ask for donations at the end," John said. "It's foolproof."

"That would be very expensive, between the staging and renting stadiums, it is overpriced. Each venue would be over two hundred thousand in cost, again blowing our budget," the accountant said.

"You do not need to sell out the biggest stadiums, target smaller ones instead," John added.

"There has to be an easier way," Commander said.

"All I need to do is get on national television by going to one place and doing an interview there. That doesn't even cost us a dime, well, other than gas money," Susan said.

"That would be easy, but where?" John asked.

"I can make some calls to get some publicity, I have a few places and people in mind. I have this one contact who literally everyone knows," Susan said.

The President of the United States was in southern California visiting the victims of a school shooting. He was under pressure because terrorism was on the rise in the United States and he was under the gun.

The president was talking to some of the young victims who were in the hospital. He was surrounded by security personnel, as protocol.

The president was tapped on the shoulder as he was talking to a parent of one of the victims.

"Sorry if you will excuse me for one moment," the president said.

"Mr. President, I have a Susan King on the line," a secret service member said to the president.

"I will talk to her in a few minutes," the president said. He did not recognize anyone by the name Susan, but once he realized it was Susan King, his priorities changed big time.

After he finished talking to the patients, he went to his large limousine that was waiting at the back of the hospital. He made sure to finish speaking to every family because he wanted to do the right thing and be human and spend his time listening to the stories in hopes of making stricter regulations.

"Is that Susan still on the phone?" the president asked the agent.

"She is, would you like to speak to her?" the agent asked.

"Yes, please," the president said.

The secret service agent handed the president the small outdated cell phone.

"Hello, President Devrai speaking," the president said.

"Hello Mister President, I was wondering if you could come to the King's Pawn to drum up publicity and to see what we are doing here?" Susan asked.

"I am in California and have a very tight schedule, I am not sure, I will let my man arrange this ... if anything," the president said.

He handed the phone to his agent who was in charge of his schedule.

"Larry speaking," Larry said.

"Hello Larry, my name ..." Susan said being interrupted.

"When do you need the president to come?" Larry asked. He wanted to get to the point as fast as possible as the president could not afford to waste time. The president spent this time talking to the front desk secretary who was thrilled to meet the president.

"As soon as he can come," Susan said.

"We can be there by around noon tomorrow," Larry said.

"That would be perfect, make sure that the news knows of this, as it would help us both," Susan said.

Larry hung up on Susan.

"Mr. President, looks like we are going to Nevada tonight," Larry said.

"Alright, I have always wanted to see this experiment that is being done. The former president was in charge of that thing and I have never seen any images or video from inside. I wonder why that is?" the president asked.

"I am unsure sir, we will find out very soon. Also, we will be bringing along two extra members from the ANSA. They want to have Susan checked and spied on because they have allegations to assume that she may be a fraud, scamming people of money and conducting a worthless experiment," Larry said.

"That is fine as long as we are safe, and the public does not know of any fraudulent actions if we were to discover them, but I don't think there will be any problems," the president said.

"Let's hope not," Larry said.

Susan was very thrilled that the president was going to visit the headquarters. He was a busy man, so she was surprised on the ease of the unexpected schedule change.

"Ladies and gentlemen, the president will be here tomorrow by noon," Susan said excitedly.

"Why?" the Commander asked.

"Well... we need some publicity and he will be the easiest, and cheapest way to get some donations ... hopefully," Susan said.

"You are just using his fame to get us money ... that's a bit sad," Derek said speaking the truth.

"We need the money and the donations. Don't forget it's for the name of science," Susan said.

"Will we take him inside the experiment?" someone asked.

"Yes, yes we will," Susan said before thinking.

"No, no we will not," Commander said correcting what Susan said.

"It is such a tremendous risk that we will not be taking," the Commander said.

"What is a risk, the president?" Susan asked.

"The fact that not only the president, but all of his security and the people would be joining him. People in the experiment would be confused and this could alter the results. We just spoke about this when you went to the occupation ceremony," the Commander said.

"I guess you have a point," Susan said. "Let's play it by ear."

Location- Los Angeles, California

The president was about to speak to a large group of people in Los Angeles about the recent attack. He also wanted to tell the world about his trip to the King's Pawn.

The president, surrounded by secret service walked onto the small stage to speak. The crowd cheered as he did. He got a loud cheer regardless of where he went. Americans just admired him, because he was one of the youngest presidents, the younger generations felt they had a deeper connection with him.

"Thank you, thank you," he said. He had to wait for the crowd to calm down.

"As you know, our country has been the center of yet another horrific attack. These attacks are just heartbreaking. We are losing countless young men and women who should be living a full life. Of these men and women some may invent the next groundbreaking cure, end poverty, find life on another planet. Sadly, none of these achievements or accomplishments can happen because we are losing the driving force as a result of violent attacks. Standing as one, as a country, we cannot and will not let this stop us from functioning. We cannot and will not let these attackers impose fear on us, the people," the president said passionately. He felt a deep passion for what he spoke about.

He was interrupted by a very loud applause from the audience that consisted of about four thousand people.

"Together we have to give aid in times of need, donate money to those without, donate more of our time, make steps in a forward direction. As the president, I have many responsibilities. National security is one of my priorities. We cannot have attacks happen to our country because I know that families are greatly affected. When families are affected, communities are affected. When communities are affected, regions follow, and when regions follow, the rest of America follows. If we prevent these threats, we will not have to worry about that downward spiral."

"Thusly, it is in the best benefit that we are increasing the security around the country and changing the gun policy to a zero tolerance. Only uniformed officers will be allowed to possess a gun. Anyone who has a gun in their possession and is caught will be arrested," the president said. The crowd cheered again.

"We have to put an end to violence and create peace out of chaos, and the only way to do that is to come together and fight back! I repeat we must fight back and speak up! Let your voices tell your thoughts! Thank you," the president said. He was speaking with such emotion a handful of onlookers thought the speech was a propaganda attempt. He dropped the microphone on the ground because he felt it was necessary.

The crowd lost their minds when he dropped the microphone and the video would go viral overnight.

The press immediately started to ask questions that the president did not feel like responding to.

"I am on a tight schedule and cannot answer questions. Feel free to join me tomorrow at noon in Nevada near the King's Pawn experiment headquarters. Due to the security status we will not be near the location, but close enough. The location of our next event tomorrow will be released to you later on today, thank you again," the president said. The press would show up by the masses in hopes to get a decent interview and news story.

His security then ushered him off the stage and away from the press members who were still trying to ask questions and into his car.

"Well done sir," Larry said.

"It was okay but I had no planned speech so I had to just improvise," the president said.

"You nailed it," Larry said.

"How did you like the microphone drop?" the president asked.

"It was amazing Mr. President," Larry said. "I am not sure that a mic drop was the right thing for a speech acknowledging a school shooting. But regardless, it was amazing."

"I kind of realized that after I dropped it," the president said.

A few minutes after the car started moving, the president continued his conversation with Larry.

"I do want a speech for tomorrow. I also want to put in a request to go into the experiment or over it, because cameras don't always show everything. I want to see the experiment in person and not from a source," the president said.

"I will work on that immediately. Although I cannot guarantee Susan will allow us inside because it is an ongoing experiment, I will try to get us as close as possible," Larry said.

"Where are we headed to now?" the president asked.

"You have a scheduled appearance on the Don Johnson Tonight Show and it happens that we are in Los Angeles, so it all works out fine," Larry said.

"Alright," the president said.

Location - Headquarters

Susan King was asked by Don Johnson to appear on his show that day. She had to get to Los Angeles by eight in the evening, so she had seven hours. She was not told that the president was also appearing at the show. The pure coincidence worked to benefit Susan and her experiment.

"So how do I get to Los Angeles in only a few hours?" Susan asked her manager.

"Well you can fly, but L.A.X. is a real pain for high status individuals. We can drive but that is very inconvenient," he said.

"Well I would much rather fly," Susan said.

"Alright, we can fly, there is a helipad on the property as you know, so why don't we get moving," he said.

"Definitely, I want some security so I can get to the studio without interruption," Susan said. "I have no time to waste."

"Yes, ma'am I understand," he said.

Susan went to John and Derek's office to speak with them.

"Gentlemen, Commander is in charge until I return. If anything of emergency status happens you can call me, emergencies only. Other than that, you shall report to Commander," Susan said.

"Sounds like a plan," John said.

Susan went to the helipad with her agent and two other bodyguards. She would need them because L.A.X. was a very busy airport.

Susan always enjoyed flying in the helicopter because it was custom designed by her, a very costly process. When she helped create the headquarters, she insisted that a helipad be built for easy travels. It did save at least a half an hour because the nearest public road was more than a half an hour away.

"So, what is the plan?" Susan asked her agent as the helicopter flew over the nearby town.

"You will speak and answer his questions. I'm assuming about your experiment. You never know what to expect from these crazy show hosts," he said.

"So true! They will ask anything to get more views or be in the news. At least Don is the most watched show, so he doesn't need to go mental to get views!" Susan said.

"That is true. Still you should be ready for anything. It doesn't hurt to be ready and prepared," he said.

"Sounds easy, can I have a glass of champagne please," Susan requested.

"Yes ma'am," he said. He grabbed a bottle out of the small refrigerator. The bottle was imported from Italy and had a face value of about three thousand dollars.

Susan drank her champagne in preparation for her big television appearance, unaware of the president, who would also be at the same event.

3:00 pm

Susan arrived at LAX at about three in the afternoon. The pilot flew very quickly and saved an hour of airtime. She would have to be escorted to her car which was waiting at the arrival area. Her two bodyguards escorted her from her helicopter on the tarmac to the entrance which took her into the airport.

When she walked through the door she was greeted by about one hundred paparazzi.

"Of course! What do you know, paparazzi are here!" Susan muttered to herself. She was not in the mood to be bothered by the annoying people who push and shove to get photos. One thing that she always thought of was how they knew which celebrities were coming through. They had pictures of anyone imaginable at hand.

Susan believed that the best way to see what someone is doing was to search them on the internet, not stalk them and pester them with questions.

"Sorry I am very late," Susan said over the choir of clicking from the cameras. The paparazzi did not buy her excuse, as it was overused.

"Dr. King, how is the experiment?" a person asked.

"It's just splendid," Susan said.

She was walking slowly because she was surrounded by people who wanted a photo and autograph. Susan did not mind the occasional autograph, but she hated the blinding lights of the cameras.

"Any new info for us?" someone asked.

"Yes, I am running late! That's my info," Susan said.

Susan did not like the situation. She did sign one autograph for a young kid. She always tried to be nice to kids because she didn't want to ignore them. She could care less about the grown adults who wanted things signed. She knew they would just sell the autograph for a fortune, and she did not approve of the corrupt industry.

"Susan, where to?" someone asked.

"Oh, I have a local television appearance," she said.

"Fancy!" some random guy yelled.

"Dude really!? Put on your big boy pants and act like a grown up!" Susan said loudly. The group laughed.

"What is going on with the budget?" someone asked. The questions were getting harder and harder as Susan inched closer and closer to the exit.

"I will be the first to say it's very low, but we are being very careful and will continue to do so," she said.

"Get them to move please," Susan said to her bodyguard.

"Ladies and gentlemen please step away from Dr. King as she is on a tight schedule and running late," the bodyguard said.

The people moved a little but not much. Susan started to walk faster so that she could try to outrun the mob following her. She also had her sunglasses on because she had eye problems from the camera flashes.

"Please move away from me," Susan said. "Common already! Go hunt someone else and stalk them!"

They listened to her and moved away. She was able to walk to her car that was waiting for her.

After what seemed like forever, she arrived at her car. She was happy to be away from the mob of people. She thought she was free, but they suddenly surrounded her car the way ants swarm a piece of food. They would do anything to get a decent photo, despite shooting through blacked out windows.

"Oh, the famous surround the car and never move trick! Totally did not expect that one!" Susan said aloud. The driver laughed.

"Alright hello sir," Susan said.

There were a few people in the black SUV. Susan, her two bodyguards and her manager were in the car.

"We will now go to the studio if these people move away from my car," the driver said.

"Sound the horn or something, we have time so do not worry," Susan said. She had lied to the paparazzi, because she was in fact a few hours early.

The driver sounded the horn and the people did not move. He started to rev the engine and the people still did not move. They were still taking photos nonstop through the very dark tinted windows.

Susan turned towards her manager and said, "Call the police because we need to get out of this."

"I can do that," the manager said.

"Until then, I will pull down the windshield sun shade cover that blocks the sun, and the people from seeing you!" the driver said.

"Thanks! Maybe these losers will actually get the hint that I do not want to be seen or bothered by them," Susan said.

"I could only imagine," the driver said.

"So, does this happen a lot?" Susan asked.

"If anyone famous is being driven, then yes all the time. But normally we start moving the car and they get out of the way. This group seems very determined," the driver said.

About five minutes later, two police cars came to the rescue. It was five minutes of people yelling and banging on the windows. The uniformed officers forced the paparazzi to move or be arrested. They moved except for one man who decided that he should jump onto the hood of the car. He was immediately tackled by the police officer and handcuffed.

The car started to move and with it came the mob. They attempted to chase it until it sped away out of range for the cameras.

"Alright now we go to the studio finally," the driver said.

"Well, wasn't that just so fun!" Susan exclaimed sarcastically.

It took a decent amount of time to get to the Hollywood Boulevard where the stars were of each of the celebrities. Susan did not have a star, but she wanted to get one badly. She could easily pay to get one put in the sidewalk, but she felt she needed to earn it legitimately.

Susan arrived at the studio well before the scheduled taping was to begin. As the black car pulled up, there was already a large crowd waiting for autographs.

"Oh no, not in the mood! I'm not dealing with this again," Susan said.

"They are organized and there is a fence that they stand behind so they cannot surround you," the driver said. He was the driver for the show, so he was familiar with the location. He personally hated the airport paparazzi, because they would do anything to get an autograph or photo. The fact that there was nothing to hold them back had a lot to do with their crazy antics.

The driver pulled the car right up to the red carpet which lead into the building.

"Wow it's like I just won an Oscar award," Susan said to the driver.

"It's funny you say that. We just put the carpet so the whole area looks more professional," the driver said.

"Well thank you for getting us here quickly," Susan said as she reached forward and handed the driver a 100 dollar bill.

"Oh, thank you so much! I am not allowed to accept tips," the driver said.

Susan reacted by opening the door of the car, leaving the driver with the money.

She smiled and whispered to her manager, "Well now he won't have to worry about accepting the tip if he has nobody to give it to."

The crowd went crazy as soon as they saw Susan. Their view was blocked by the two bodyguards. They did not know Susan King was going to be on the show. They were expecting the president, but Susan was a very big surprise.

"Susan, over here please," a guy shouted. Before she knew it, all of the people were yelling to get her attention. She put her sunglasses on and walked right past them as if they were nonexistent. They were all very angry.

"Oh, my bad. I am 'running a bit late' sorry," Susan said sarcastically as she walked past the crowd.

"That is what they all say," an angry person yelled.

"Well looks like I joined another great club! The everyone club. It feels great to be a part," Susan said comically. She was known to have a rude sense of humor by ignoring people.

"You are not late! The show doesn't start for hours! You can sign some!" someone yelled.

"You are right, I could, but I don't want to! I want to relax for a while away from you and your friends!" Susan said. She had a crude sense of humor. She loved to humiliate and upset people she did not know.

A medium sized man with brown hair greeted Susan at the door.

"Doctor King, thank you for being here. Mr. Johnson would like to speak to you in his office," the man said.

"Sounds fine, I am honored to be here," Susan said. Susan followed the man to the office. She did not think much of the building because she was used to a very elegant office. She was disgusted by the cheapness of the interior. She knew that it was designed to look expensive, but they used cheap materials to fake the look.

"Alright ma'am, here is his office," the man said.

"Thanks," Susan said.

"My pleasure," the man said. Susan knocked on the door with the letter DJ and she heard a voice say enter.

She opened the door and was greeted by Don Johnson. He was a taller man, with blonde hair and a very famous smile. His show was the most popular late-night show on television. He had met nearly every A-list Hollywood actor and actress and had most of the popular bands on his show.

"Hello Dr. King, thank you so much for being here in such a short time," Don said.

"I am glad to be here. The public has not heard from me in a bit, so it is a nice surprise for them too," Susan said. Don did not know how to respond so he continued what he wanted to say.

"A quick rundown, basically you will be coming on at about nine, so one hour after we start. After the band Glaizers plays, we will go to a break, then you will come out and we will talk live. I will have another guest with you at the same time," Don said.

"Wait... who is this guest you speak of?" Susan asked.

"I do not know, I will not know until two minutes before the segment because we have not heard back from their agents yet," Don said. He was telling a lie, he knew very well that the president was going to be on, he wanted Susan and the president to talk because he figured the viewers would enjoy the duo.

"So how is the experiment?" Don asked to quickly change the subject of their conversation.

"It's going good, that's what I can say," Susan said.

Meanwhile the president was finishing up a lunch with some old friends downtown before the show. He was looking forward to going to the King's Pawn experiment. He first had to go to the Don Johnson show.

The secret service went to the studio well before the president to map it out and find exits. They also needed to find a way to get the president in and out without many people seeing. It was their job to eliminate as many situations as possible. To do that, they would have to go to the parking lot behind the studio that is gated off by a concrete wall. Then they would have to walk the president inside. They were using three SUVs in Los Angeles because they did not want to draw attention to his regular limousine. The SUV was protected by heavy armor, but less noticeable.

After the lunch, the president was escorted to his car where he would be driven ten minutes to the studio.

"So, what am I going to be talking about?" the president asked Larry.

"Just what's going on in the country. I presume that Don will mention the recent spike in terrorism," Larry said.

"Let's hope not, because I am tired of talking about negative things, there are never positive things in this world to talk about," the president said.

"I agree with you, there are not enough positive things," Larry said.

"Well the positive things don't make it to the public eye. All they see is late night shows, celebrity scandals, shootings, attacks, and sports. Nothing good is ever publicized," the president said.

"Right! The media does that because they know people are interested and would want to know about sports and big scandals. People are nosy," Larry said.

"It's just human instinct to wonder more about what everyone else is doing, more than what you are doing," the president said.

"How far away are we?" the president asked.

"Well approximately five minutes sir," Larry said.

"Also, we are going through the parking garage to avoid the public for your safety," Larry said.

"Alright," the president said.

The three-car motorcade pulled up to the parking garage one minute apart from each other to lessen suspicion that three black cars raise entering the same place. The president's car was the first and then the other two followed.

The president walked into the building where the same man who greeted Susan was waiting. Nobody saw him get out of the car and walk fifty feet to the door.

"Hello Mr. President! Very nice to meet you," he said as he offered his hand for a handshake.

"Nice to meet you also. How are you?" the president asked.

"I am fantastic, Mr. Johnson would like to speak to you in his office, if that is alright," he said.

"Definitely, let's go," the president said.

The president was followed by a very large army of secret service agents, most of whom were already inside the building waiting for his arrival.

They arrived at the office that already had two security guards standing outside the door.

"Hello Don," the president said before he opened the door.

Don greeted the president at the door.

"Wow hello Mr. President, I am beyond honored to have you here. I know you are such a busy man," Don said.

"Indeed, I am, but nobody said the president can't have a little fun from time to time," the president said.

"We all need to enjoy ourselves!" Don said.

"Would you mind signing our wall?" Don asked.

"Yes, I would mind," the president said sarcastically.

The wall on the left side of the wooden desk was filled with signatures of different people in different colors and sizes. Some of the signatures included the late Rolling Stones, the late Paul McCartney from the Beatles, and many different actors. There was one signature that Don really loved having. That of the head of the biggest human experiment in history, Susan King. The president failed to notice the odd-looking signature with a large chess piece.

"Why?" Don asked.

"I am joking with you! I would love to sign the wall," the president said.

"Thank you so much!" Don said to the president.

"It's no problem," the president replied.

"So, what is your favorite part about being president?" Don asked.

"I honestly love meeting world leaders and setting up younger generations to a good future," the president said.

"That must be a cool part," Don said.

"I also love to travel," the president said.

"Me too, I can't get enough time to travel because I am here doing what I love," Don said.

"When I travel, I am constantly surrounded by secret service, often so many of them that they created a wall I can't see over, and when I am on vacation, they shut down the beach and areas around me," the president said.

"That must be terrible," Don said.

"It is! I can't even go to a private beach without a big operation! At least you can travel and only have to sign things and take photos. You can then enjoy your trip. I can't really enjoy it because I am never truly alone," the president said.

"It is better to be safe than sorry," Don said.

"I do not like shutting down places if I do not have to, but I am forced to," the president said.

"The only place I shut down is any restaurant or store I walk into," Don said. He was partially joking, but often his presence creates such a frenzy, that the place is forced to shut down until he leaves.

"You can wait in the lounge or wherever the security deems safe, because the filming starts in a bit. Thank you again Mr. President," Don said.

"My pleasure," the president replied.

Chapter Nineteen

The Don Johnson show was very popular in the United States. At nine in the evening, the show started. It was nine o'clock in California and the show began.

"He is the best host on television, star of The Don Johnson tonight show, sir Don Johnson!" the announcer said. Nobody knew who this man was, because he had never been named or showed. His voice was very recognizable though. He was referred to as Nate sometimes, but his real name was Nathan.

The crowd cheered loudly as Don walked out onto the set wearing a very expensive black suit, that he had custom made. He had changed out of jeans and a t-shirt just before the show started.

On the Set of the TV Show

"Thank you everyone! thanks," he said. The crowd was still applauding loudly. All of a sudden when Don started to talk, the crowd silenced themselves. The secret was the director told the people when to applaud and when to stop. He was just off the view of the camera along with the thirty secret service members.

"So tonight, we have a huge show. Break the news! Tell them who is going to be here Nate," Don said.

"Alrighty Don! Tonight, we have the founder and head of the King's Pawn experiment, Doctor Susan King in studio. We have the up and coming band Glaizers here to perform their number one top selling song Sentellation. We have President Jonathan Devrai live in studio and so many more!" Nate said.

"So to start off, each week we insert me into the top moments of the week. It's 'Don does Everything,'" Don said.

The segment named "Don Does Everything" is a very popular weekly segment. The editors take the big moments of the week and either edit Don's voice over that of the actual person talking or overlay a video of Don's head over the person talking. It made for a rather entertaining segment. Don never gave the editors proper credit because they made the video look like Don was actually in the video rather than being edited into the video.

People started laughing during the video as the viewers were watching the segment. The video played live in the studio so the audience could enjoy it.

"What many of you do not know is how hard it is to make these 'Don Does Everything' segments. Our editors work long hours to find and edit me into the videos. On average they spend about thirty hours a week making one segment. So, give them a hand ... C'mon America, I can see you sitting on the couch not cheering," Don said.

The crowd applauded for the editors. Even the editors watching from the back room were cheering because they were happy to finally be acknowledged.

"I now invite a young boy on stage, Antoine. He submitted a video to us ... well, let him do the explaining," Don said as he put his hand on his closed laptop, his cue to the director to start the video.

The video of Antoine started playing. He was a seven-year-old boy who loved President Devrai.

"Hello Mr. Johnson, my name is Antoine. I am seven years old and I live in Seattle, Washington. If I could ask President Devrai any question I would ask him 'What do you know that we do not?'" said the young boy.

"Well Antoine, please come out and join me," Don said.

The crowd cheered for the young boy who looked excited to be in the studio walked out to Dons couch.

"Thank you, it is so nice to meet you," Antoine said.

"My honor, you deserved it," Don said. The crowd clapped after Don finished his handshake.

"So, Antoine, what inspired your question?" Don asked.

"Well I wanted to know what the government is hiding from us. We learned about conspiracies in school, and I wanted to see if I would be able to solve one for America ... So, I wanted to ask the president," Antoine said.

"That is really cool," Don said. "Did you ever think you would be on a television show?"

"Not in a million years," Antoine said.

"Alright, well here to answer your question please welcome President Jonathan Devrai," Don said. Everyone loved how Don was able to make interviews with anyone seem so laid back and conversational. That was a talent that made him very successful.

The crowd went wild and so did Antoine. His dream was to meet the president, and it was about to come true.

"Thank you for being here Mr. President," Don said as he reached out to shake the president's hand.

"My pleasure," the president said.

"This is Antoine from Seattle and he wants to ask you a question," Don said.

"Nice to meet you Antoine," the president said.

"So, I heard you have a question for me," the president said.

"I do! But it is so cool to meet you" Antoine said excitedly.

"It is really cool to meet you too buddy! Well let's hear your question," the president said.

"I was wondering what you know that regular Americans don't?" Antoine asked.

"Wow that is a tough question. Well, there is so much you don't know, but I can't say most of it. Is there anything in specific you wonder about?" the president asked. He did not expect such a punch to the gut with a huge question from a little kid.

"There is a pawn experiment ... I have only heard of it once," Antoine said.

"To be honest, even as president I don't know very much about it. I know nothing more than you do, mainly because the former president along with congress agreed to have it be done here in the United States," the president said.

"Are there aliens in Area 51?" Antoine asked. The crowd and Don laughed.

"Yikes! I did not see that one coming. Do you know why nobody knows if there are aliens in Area 51?" the president asked Antoine.

"Because nobody has been inside it," Antoine said.

"Well that is true, but there is another reason. The government is dedicated to public," the president said as he was interrupted by a random guy.

"It's because the government is a joke! You are a joke! You are just too afraid to tell us the truth!" the guy yelled. He was taken out by security.

"In response to that gentleman, I am not afraid to tell the public the truth. Rather we conceal the truth because the public reaction to the truth can be dangerous and can lead to things we don't want, if that makes sense," the president said. Antoine was still next to the president.

"So, Mr. President, what is the toughest decision you have made so far?" Antoine asked.

"Wow! That is a good question. Every one of my choices is not easy to make, often they are stressful. The choices I do make I have to think of the consequences and outcomes of making them. I think what would happen if I changed this or that," the president said.

"Branching off of that, was there any decision that you regret making?" Don asked.

"There are always a few screw ups that you wish you never made, but I really do not have one particular example," the president said.

"Wow! The way you handled that was amazing! But, sadly, we have to go to break!" Don said.

During the break, the president signed a few items for Antoine and spoke with some people in the audience. He was really a down to earth guy when the situation was calm enough to interact with people.

"We are back and I have the president with me. So, Mr. President, what is the funniest thing you have done to someone?" Don asked.

"Well, um, I have done some pretty funny things. Oh yes I have a good one. I have walked to public shops despite my security denying it. That causes a mass freakout in the security office. Like you don't understand the sheer level of freakout … it's out of this world. Another time I was on vacation in Europe at a pizza shop when I overheard a young girl talking to her mom about me. She didn't know I was right behind her in line. I took a selfie standing behind her and then tapped on her shoulder. She turned and froze. Her mom thought I was a creep and hit me with her purse, then she realized I was the president of the United States. My security almost tackled her to the ground, but I stopped them. That was a good time," the president said.

"Wow the things you do!" Don said. "Those ruthless secret service, it's just a purse. Seriously, there will not be bricks in the purse of some lady in a pizza shop."

The crowd laughed.

"Don, I am sure you have done some funny things to people also. It just comes with the fame," the president said. He wanted Don to share some stories.

"I have ... I love to prank and scare people. Their reactions are priceless. Oh, one time I went to a Dodgers game and ran onto the field. All of the police came running after me. It took them some time to realize it was me, but when they did their demeanor changed, they became friendly. Friendly as in I didn't get tackled to the ground quite as painfully," Don said. The studio audience, many of them from Los Angeles, laughed because they remembered vividly when Don did the stunt without first telling the authorities.

"So, what's the biggest perk being the president has?" Don asked.

"Well, there are tons of perks. I like the fact that I can get anything hand delivered whenever I want, or I can give my men heart attacks at a moment's decision. I just love to *spice* things up a bit, no pun intended," the president said.

"How do you do that?" Don asked.

"By asking to stop the motorcade convoy to walk in public in places that may not be safe. It causes them to freak out a bit," the president said.

"I freak my security army out too, like the time we had a fake attacker in the audience. I didn't tell them that the dude who was pretending to attack me was an actor. He may or may not have been injured and carried out by the medics," Don said. The crowd laughed because they enjoyed the fact that a staged scene was the best story Don had to share.

"Oh wait! We have a clip of the incident for you to see!" Don said.

The clip was exactly what Don described it to be.

After the clip was finished, the interview continued.

"But see for instance I can do this," the president said.

He got up and walked towards the audience. His security service agents started to go towards the audience to keep the audience away from the president. It was protocol to put their body in between the president and the people, even though the crowd was very calm and still in their seats. The sound of ten suits starting to move was clearly audible as they got into formation blocking a few cameras in the process.

"So, who wants to get a photo with me?" the president asked the crowd.

They went crazy. Everyone wanted the rare chance to take a selfie with the president, especially because they would be on television.

"I'm kidding," the president said. The crowd collaboratively created a sigh that was loud enough for viewers at home to hear.

He walked back to his seat by Don, who was laughing at the chaos in his studio.

"That's what they hate," the president said.

"I could imagine it be a bit stressful for them. But they are keeping you safe, even though most instances are safe, it's better to be safe than miss the one threat," Don said.

"Yes, that is true. They keep me safe so I can do my job without any unwanted visitors," the president said.

"Speaking of stressful, this next guest has worked tediously for the last 15 years. She probably has the most stressful job on earth. Nate, do it!" Don said energetically.

"Ladies and gentlemen please welcome Doctor Susan King," Nate said with his famous voice.

The crowd cheered because Susan had never been on a late night show. She walked out to the desk and waved to the audience.

"Welcome," Don said.

"Hello Mr. President," Susan said to the president as they shook hands and hugged. The hug was more for show, because Susan knew the president pretty well.

"Nice to meet you Susan," the president said.

"So Susan, wow, I am unable to say how honored I am to have you on my show," Don said.

"Thanks Don, but that's a little much," Susan said.

"Speaking of conspiracies and stress, how is the project?" Don asked.

"Well it is going good right now, there is not much I can disclose to you, but I can say I have been super busy with things," Susan said.

"Yep, it's sort of like Area 51, I know what is inside. Secrets are kept by the government because of public reaction if they were released," the president said to back what Susan said.

"So, what do you actually do as the head of the King's Pawn?" Don asked.

"I actually created and started this whole thing. It took years to start because getting approval was nearly impossible. During the day, I watch the live feed and we talk in the headquarters about what is going on, and if any new information is shown. I act just as the Chief Executive Officer of a major corporation does, except my corporation is an active scientific experiment that costs more than the NASA space program," Susan said.

"Sounds tedious. So, what have you been doing lately?" Don asked.

"It is tedious, we have to literally watch people live... it is fun trust me! To answer your question, I have traveled the country to raise awareness for a critical aspect of my experiment," Susan said.

"What may that be?" Don asked.

"We are asking for donations of the remains of people who have passed. In the society there is a medical need for deceased. We will bury them in a very proper burial," Susan said.

"Where can people donate a body?" Don asked in a way that showed he did not believe what he was saying. He never expected to ask people how to donate a body on national television.

"Well, tomorrow the president and I will be in Nevada and I will specify in detail how you can donate," Susan said.

"Why have you not told the public more factual information about your experiment?" Don asked.

"Well mainly it is a security issue and secondly the concepts in which we are conducting research on are very delicate and we don't want the wrong people getting hold of it. And also what the president said moments ago about the reaction is true. Most importantly, we are conducting scientific research, as it is ongoing, we cannot tell the public information that is only assumed," Susan said.

"Is there more to it than that? It cannot be that simple... no way!" the president asked.

"Yes ... no, no there's really not, if you were the head of a multi-billion, not million but a billion dollar experiment, you would sweat everything imaginable. If I mess this up, not only my life will be ruined but my reputation will be horrible," Susan said.

"Well I am the head of the United States, and my reputation won't be ruined," the president said. He was trying to be funny, but his comment came off as being more rude.

"Let's say you cause bankruptcy for millions of people because your spending cost billions, do you think that anyone would trust you ever again with a loan or anything for that matter?" Susan asked.

"Likely not," the president said.

"Likely exactly. That's my point," Susan said.

"Also imagine that you spent over twenty years doing one thing and nothing but. You have to regulate living people and if one of them does wrongfully you are charged with murder... it's very difficult," Susan said.

"I am in charge and in control of over one hundred million people," the president said.

"I understand it, but the hardest thing is that I may be able to disprove every logical neuron in the human brain," Susan said.

"Well I disprove conspiracies too," the president said.

"Alright so what one thing do you wish you could change?" Don asked. He needed to regain control of the two high status individuals. He knew that their argument would make great television.

"About what?" Susan asked.

"About your life, about anything," Don said.

"I wish I had not done one thing, one very big mistake that I will not say, but I know it will be my tragic flaw if not other things first," Susan said.

"What do you mean?" Don said.

"I mean that as a human, we all make mistakes. I have made many mistakes both out of impulsivity and selfishness. I understand that nobody is perfect not even myself. I also realize that the things I have done are wrong and will most likely ruin my life. My message to people is think before you do things because you have to realize the effect down the road," Susan said.

"Very good message," Don said.

"Well I have not done anything too bad ... yet, but you never know what happens tomorrow right?" the president said.

The crowd laughed.

Chapter Twenty

Susan had made many mistakes in her life. Her biggest was stealing money from the experiment. In reality she did not make a lot of money from her experiment. She knew that going into it, but she also knew that if her experiment worked, she would become one of the wealthiest people alive. She also realized that the experiment would take over fifteen years so she needed instant money.

She started the experiment with a decent budget, and the inherited money from her father. She soon ran into unseen problems that cost a lot of money. She received large donations from some of the richest people which significantly helped her cause. But her human greed became too much. She had a net worth of 750,000 dollars mainly because of her father's one million dollar estate. Other than the estate she had virtually no spending money. She started out buying small things for herself with the money. Things like cars, offices, clothing, vehicles, and publicity. She purchased many black SUV's that she had custom designed. She built a lavish headquarter for the project at nearly five times the original budget. The original plans for the headquarters were estimated at two million dollars, but by the end of her "small" changes were estimated at ten million dollars.

She issued a salary increase for not only herself, but for John, Derek and the Commander. She would be making 1,790,000 dollars per year, which was much more than she needed. John and Derek made 700,000 dollars each, up from 250,000 dollars. The Commander made just over one million dollars per year.

In addition, Susan was making money from publicity and sponsorships. She was approached by large name brand companies including Ford, which she signed to. She could get money from nearly anyone she met who had money to spend because she was great at negotiations.

She had to be careful because she realized that she could be sued for fraud because she was taking money for herself from a government project. She stopped taking money after she increased her net worth to over ten million dollars.

She was nearly arrested twice for traffic violations and tax evasion. She was bailed out by the Queen.

When Don Johnson asked Susan what she would change, she immediately thought of her past. The times she stole millions of dollars. It was at that time she realized she needed to be very careful because the experiment relied on her. If she went down, she would make sure that she brings down the King's Pawn with her because she was a greedy human being.

Chapter Twenty-One

I was in the second week of my new occupation as the Chief Elder. I found enjoyment in the tests he did to me through the device. Some were of better status than others. Some I never wanted to do again, and others I wanted to do again.

The Chief Elder also was educating me on how to drive a rac. It was not easy at first, but I found it easier and easier each time I did it.

The first time I drove was with the device. I was sitting in a chair, a real one with two pedals and a wheel. I was on a street that was straight, with no buildings on either side. There were other racs coming towards me on the other side of the road. I pressed the pedal on the right in relation to the other pedal. The rac started to move. As I pressed the pedal harder, the rac moved faster.

"Careful the maximum speed one can travel per hour of duration is twenty-two," a voice said.

I looked at the speed measure and I realized my rac was moving at thirty-eight. I pressed the other pedal and the rac stopped abruptly. The jolt from the friction was more powerful than I was expecting. I had to remember to hit the left pedal less than the adjacent one.

The rac was still moving, I had to maintain a constant speed over distance ratio with the rac. I did that by keeping the amount of pressure on the right pedal equal over a long period of time, so the rac continued to move not faster or slower.

I noticed that the rac was moving a good deal of distance since sixteen other racs had passed mine.

"Now the limit of duration per hour is sixty-two," the voice said.

I pressed the pedal harder and the rac gained speed very quickly.

"Test terminated," the voice said.

I was back in the testing room.

"You did very good," the Chief Elder said.

"Did I pass?" I asked.

"You did, now we will go in my rac on the street, act the same and you will do just fine," he said.

We went to his rac which was different than the one my family possessed. His was a small fraction larger, but I noticed.

"Your rac is bigger than ours," I said.

"It is a special rac that only the Chief Elder can drive," he said.

"What makes it special?" I asked.

"You have an inquisitive young mind, it has some machines that assist me to drive because it can be difficult because of my age," he said.

I was looking around the interior of the rac and I noticed a blue circle with four different looking letters of some sort.

"What is this?" I asked pointing to the circular object.

"I do not know," he said.

"What does it read?" I asked.

"It reads 'Ford Company'" he said.

"What is that?" I asked.

"It is the production of our rac, it is where they are produced," he said.

"You may get to see it someday," he continued.

"Cool," I said.

"Now you will press the right pedal just like the test and we will turn right out of the rac house," he said.

"Alight," I said.

I pressed the right pedal and turned the wheel to the right to turn the rac.

"Great now the limit of speed here is sixteen, so let see where this street goes," he said.

The buildings were passing us at an almost even pattern. Mainly because each of the buildings were the same distance apart from each other. We continued to move on the same street, until I saw the turn ahead.

"Let's continue our path do not turn left," he said.

The society was getting farther behind us. There were mountains very far ahead, ones that had imperfections and impurities. They were built naturally and I loved the unsymmetrical conformity of them.

"There will be a turn in six minutes of time, it circles the entire society and we can go any speed it will be a good practice for you," he said.

I was looking forward to moving faster because as a youth I was never given the freedom of such grace.

The turn was approaching rapidly.

"Slow down a little and make the turn then accelerate," he said.

I did as he was instructing. I made a very sharp turn because I started turning too late. I hit the left pedal hard as a natural reaction to avoid driving off the road. The rac jolted strongly.

"I apologize I made a mistake," I said.

"It is okay, you are young and will learn to make clean maneuvers with the rac," he said.

"Now the speed is whatever you want, there will be no other racs here as nobody but you and myself know about this," he said.

The road went straight for a while. The land seemed to pass by as time goes, unnoticed. My speed increased as numbers increase without reasoning.

I became at one with the surrounding mountains and grounds. I became encased in the complication of time to the point I became unaware that I was still driving.

"You have been driving on this road for twelve minutes," he said. His voice caught me off guard as I was in some sort of trance.

"What was I just experiencing?" I asked.

"You were experiencing joy and freedom as you have you never before. Freedom is a rarity in our society, the only freedom I have is driving and my decisions which impact the freedom of the rest," he said.

"Well I like driving and I like freedom," I said.

"Most do, there are not many who do not like freedom, but you mustn't let freedom overcome you. Most will never experience freedom," he said.

"What do you mean?" I asked.

"In society, people are given little freedom. On the Gifted Day, people have freedom under limitations. As a member of society it is your responsibility to make choices that are the right ones. When you make bad decisions you have punishment. It is only you who claims responsibility for yourself. If you make a bad choice you have only yourself to blame. As the Chief Elder, I have to think very deeply to make a decision because it will not only affect me, but it will affect everyone in our society. That is what you have yet to experience," he said.

"When will I experience it?" I asked.

"Very soon, in the coming time. I will teach you how to make the decisions the best you can," he said.

"I want you to drive to your LOO right now because you will get your possessions and bring them to my LOO where you will reside as my assistant and eventually you will succeed me," he said.

"Alright," I said. I drove the rac to my LOO. It seemed like no time had passed. My LOO was very lonely, very still, almost eerie. Due to the time of the day, my mom and dad were at their occupations, my sister was at hers.

"I will be waiting in the rac for your return. Take your possessions from your sleeping quarters and return to the rac," he said.

"Alright," I said.

I went to the door that kept my family in, and it was open. The Code stated that the door is to remain open at all times. Members in our society never stole from others because everyone had the same possessions and had no reason to take from others.

I went to my sleeping quarters and it was as I expected. My bed was made to perfection as it always was. I grabbed my large travel case that was used for moving many items. I filled it with my possessions and took it back to the rac. The process was difficult because my family was important to me. I loved them, and it was difficult for me to reside apart from them. I would not have anyone to talk to on a family level. I would have no sister to play games with and talk to. I lost it all with my occupation, but becoming such a high status member was worth it. After all, I was still able to visit family and talk to them, just not live with them.

I had my few books, of which some I had read and others I had not. My mom gave me a few of them when I was younger.

I had a copy of The Code which I read quite often. I also had a game called the Pawns Strategy. It was a game where the goal is to put the oppositions King in a position where it could not be moved. It was called checkmate. I enjoyed the game because I liked using logic to solve problems. I had only lost the first time I played the game.

When I got back to the rac with my possessions, the Chief Elder was sitting in the driver's seat. I put my possessions in the back of the rac and then I sat in the side adjacent to that of the Chief Elder.

"Did you put all your possessions in my rac?" he asked.

"Yes," I said.

"Alright, so now we go to my LOO. You have never been there, but rather we were at my occupation room. My LOO is larger than yours as it will house both of us. It also has a training room and a few others," he said.

"I think I have seen your LOO," I said.

"It is very likely," he said.

"So, the following day we will be gaining knowledge about a thing called Science. You will gain knowledge about the general aspects, because I feel it is best for you to know about more than just how to make decisions," he said.

"I have gained knowledge about science at the Education Center," I said.

"You have, but I will tell you more," he said.

"Where do you get your knowledge from?" I asked.

"Well I am unsure, I just know this information. You will be responsible for making decisions like I was for years," he said.

I found it odd that he did not know where he gained his knowledge from.

The Next Day

The LOO was in fact bigger than the one my family owned. His had more items and a different flow to it. Each room flowed into the next, unlike my families LOO which rooms were clearly separated.

His LOO had three levels which was unusual. I went to consume food early in the morning. To my surprise, he was already making the food.

"Well good morning to you," he said.

"Good morning," I said.

"How was your room?" he asked.

"I liked my sleeping quarters," I said.

"Your room you liked it?" he asked.

I had never heard the word room instead of sleeping quarters.

"I loved my ... my room, it was very different. My room at my LOO was much smaller in size," I said

"That is true, my LOO is much larger," he said. "Call it home from now on. You will learn that the proper term is home or house, so try to be more formal."

"After you eat, we will begin," he said.

"Alright," I said.

I finished eating and I was eager to begin learning.

"So now I will show you some simple science," he said.

"I'm ready," I said.

He took me to a room very similar to the one at the other location, if not the same room. The same device was there.

He put the device on my head and it began.

"Conventional Biology: the Theory of Evolution. Alpha, Beta and Gamma Radiation Decay, Radioisotopes," the voice said.

I did not know what to do. I also did not realize that this was a decision test to see how I would react in a given scenario.

I assumed I needed to choose one of the odd amounts. The first one I had knowledge on. The second one I had never seen before. The final one I assumed to be a radioactive isotope which I had knowledge on.

"Alpha, beta, gamma radiation," I said.

"Alpha decay also to be alluded to as helium nucleus, is the weakest form of radiation. A Beta radiation particle is an electron and is moderate in strength. Gamma is the strongest and has no mass," a voice said.

I had to figure out what to do next. All of the terms were written on a wall. I was confused as to what to do.

"What do I do now?" I asked.

"You make a decision," the voice said.

"I chose already what I wanted to acquire knowledge on," I said.

"Very well then, terminating today's test," the voice said.

I was back in the home of the Chief Elder.

"How was it?" he asked.

"It was tough to make a decision," I said.

"Yes, but your decision will affect the entire society," he said.

"At the end I was confused," I said.

"You often will be left without a definitive solution or choice," he said.

"What was I supposed to do next?" I asked.

"I cannot tell you, but you will learn over time and discover the solution," he said.

"What do we do now?" I asked.

"I want you to obtain knowledge about a topic I do not know a lot about ... psychology," he said.

I had heard the word before in education, but I was unable to recall what it meant.

"It is a crucial aspect to my position as the Chief Elder," he said.

"Ok," I said.

We went to the room where the device was and it began.

I was in a room with a large object on a square screen. This object was very odd because it was not perfect ... and the hue was very abnormal. It was in some way, a form of solid red, but not as solid.

"This is a brain ... a vital ... the most vital part of the human body," a voice said stressing the word most.

"Ok," I said. I was wondering who humans were.

"Who are human?" I asked.

"All the members of society are human and so are you," the voice said.

"So, I am a human?" I asked.

"You are a human, yes," the voice said. I had never heard the word human. I had only heard members of society, which must be a name for human.

"The term psychology means the study of the brain. Sociology is the study of how one's brain processes thoughts," the voice said. The voice stopped talking ...

"I want to know about psychology," I said because the Chief Elder had mentioned psychology.

"There are many different parts of the human brain. When looking at the brain, the left side is responsible for the right side of the body. The right side of the brain is responsible for the left side of the body," the voice said.

I was confused why that was ...

"Why?" I asked.

"It is very complex ... you do not need to worry too much about why... rather just know the fact," the voice said.

"To continue, there are many different parts of the brain, many cortices, the plural form of cortex. The cerebrum, ethornial, are just two of the cortices," the voice said.

"What do they do?" I asked.

"They control you," the voice said.

I was again confused how something can control me.

"What do you mean?" I asked.

"They control all of your human functions. Your brain processes your thoughts and signals nerves to move muscles, and other body parts. Without a brain you could not do anything... you could not live," the voice said.

"But everything is possible," I said.

"Well actually you can live without a brain. It is a very rare disorder from another society in which one is born without the brain. It is called Anencephaly in the other societies. The key is the brain stem which is responsible for breathing and other automatic body functions. This person without the brain cannot do anything but breathe and eat with assistance, so technically it is not living," the voice said.

"Wow," I said.

"Why does our society not have that?" I asked.

"It's extremely rare, only a few people have ever had that case, and none of them reside in your society," the voice said.

"Psychology also deals with understanding why people do things or do not do things," the voice said.

I was trying to think of what the voice was saying.

"For example, as the Chief Elder you may be faced with problems that do not seem right. It will be your job to solve the problem that may not be an easy one. If somebody commits a crime against the code that is punishable by banishment, you will have to make the decision to banish or condemn or execute," the voice said.

"Then I would be a killer," I said.

"No, YOU would not be the killer, YOU would be the person behind the killing," the voice said emphasizing you.

"What should I do in that situation?" I asked.

"Make a decision. It ties back to psychology because you have to think about how does this decision affect myself or the society," the voice said.

"You will have to find out why they did what they did, what their state of mind is ... you can do this through by reversing their logic through questioning," the voice said.

"What would I ask?" I asked.

"You will discover soon enough ... you will know when the time has come ..." the voice said.

Chapter Twenty-Two

Susan King got back to the Nevada based headquarters very early in the morning. She was exhausted from the ordeal in California.

The Don Johnson show ended at ten. Susan arrived to the airport by eleven. She did not have to battle with too many paparazzi, but there were enough. The majority of them were outside the studio by her car.

She boarded the same helicopter at 11:09 at night.

"Can I have a drink please?" Susan asked lazily.

"Yes, Mrs King, would you like wine?" the guard asked.

"Yes, that will do," Susan said. She loved to drink wine after busy situations because she thought it helped to calm down. In reality it did not help at all.

"How did it go: the show?" the guard asked.

"I think it went fine, I didn't get asked tough questions," Susan said.

"I was watching it and it looked like you enjoyed yourself," the guard said.

"I did it was pretty fun," Susan said.

"When was the last time you were on a show?" the guard asked.

"It has been a really long time," Susan said.

"It felt great to get a break from my stressful job," Susan said.

"I could only imagine how tough your job is ma'am," the guard said.

"It's tough, really tough," Susan said.

Susan arrived at the headquarters well into the next morning. She was exhausted from her all-nighter.

The Commander and John were the only ones at the headquarters. Derek would be coming into the headquarters in a few hours. It was very early in the morning before sunrise. The president was due to arrive later in the day.

"Hello everyone," Susan said loudly.

John came out of his office.

"Hello Dr. King. How was the show?" he asked.

"It was great," Susan replied.

"I watched it on television. Did you know the president would be there too?" John asked.

"No, I did not. I was not too pleased by that surprise, but I did enjoy myself," Susan said.

"That is good. Luckily nothing happened here that was too important," John said.

"Well everything is important... but I understand what you mean," Susan said.

"Why don't you go get some sleep and get ready for the president because it's really early," John said.

"Sounds like a plan. If anything happens you know to call me," Susan said.

"Yep sure thing," John said.

"One more thing ... do you know when he will be here?" Susan asked.

"I am not sure. I think sometime in the afternoon, but he is the president and his schedule can change in an instant," John said.

"Alright ... I am going to go home then grab some breakfast in the town. See you in a bit. And where is Derek?" Susan asked.

"He is resting but he will be here after the sun rises so we can both be on hand for the president," John said.

"Alright," Susan said.

Susan was exhausted but she wanted to go into town to get some breakfast because she had not done so in a long time.

She was driven to her work house by a driver who managed to avoid any collisions. The work house was built near the headquarters so Susan could go home and rest easily, while being near work. She changed clothes, took a shower, and redid her hair so she looked presentable.

After about an hour, she left for the city. The nearest city was about ten minutes by car from her house ... the house near headquarters. She had a home in Las Vegas, but she rarely ever used it due to her job. She had homes all over the

The King's Pawn

United States, but she rarely used any of them because she never had time off.

As she was being driven through the city, she kept noticing a lot of press.

"Are they here for the president?" Susan asked the driver.

"I believe so ma'am," the driver said.

"Why though, there are a million much easier locations to meet the president," Susan said.

"Yes, but again this is the first time he has ever been to your experiment... it is huge news," the driver said.

"The restaurant is up here," Susan said.

"Yes, I see it," the driver said.

"Do we have any security?" Susan asked.

"You do Dr. King, they are in the car behind us," the driver said.

"Great!" Susan said.

As the two black SUV's approached the only restaurant in the small town with a population of around 15,000, people started to notice the cars really quickly.

"Thank you," Susan said.

"My pleasure ma'am," the driver said.

Susan walked into the restaurant and it was packed with people, every one of them with a cameraman.

Susan also knew she had security, but she did not make the connection that there would be tons of media people inside the restaurant. Susan wore clothes that she thought would help her look like a reporter. She wanted to blend in as much as she possibly could.

"How many people?" the waiter asked.

"One please, away from the media if possible," Susan said.

"Is the window booth fine?" the waiter asked.

"Yes, it will do," Susan said.

She was looking at the menu while sitting in a small booth. Her security guards were sitting on the outside of the booth so that they were able to block people from getting to Susan.

"This place is too noisy and too dirty," Susan said.

"I agree," a bodyguard said. "It is the only place for food other than at the headquarters or your home."

"Well I guess this will do. Don't you want something to eat?" Susan asked.

"No ma'am, we are not here to enjoy, we are here to keep you safe," a bodyguard said. She got them some coffee and a small pancake.

Susan was looking out the window at the street. There were some shops, and a jewelry store. It was the main block of the town, Main Street. It was blocked off by the police because there was a stage being set up. The television reporters gained their territory and kept it from competitors. The street was lined with various news vans.

A young man, who Susan secretly thought was good looking turned and noticed her. This young man was the head reporter for ABC evening news. He immediately recognized Susan, and in no time, he was headed toward the window.

Meanwhile, inside the restaurant another reporter was doing a live coverage segment talking about Susan.

"Um I do not know if Dr. King will come out and speak at this moment," the reporter said.

"Um ..." the reporter said a few seconds later as he turned around and saw Susan.

"Yes Dr. King is here right now, you are right," the reporter said.

At that point, every reporter within fifteen feet turned towards Susan.

"Well that was short lived," Susan whispered.

They all came towards her table at once. Even outside reporters noticed the hubbub going on inside the restaurant.

All of the cameramen moved their camera to try to get a view of Susan.

"Dr. King," a reporter said.

"Susan what do you think," another reporter said.

"Suuuusssaaan," a random guy yelled very loudly. He was sitting at the small bar, not surprising based on his behavior.

It was all a blob to Susan, she could not hear a specific voice but a crowd. Reporters were shoving microphones in her direction. She could not move because her table was surrounded.

"Give us space," one of her bodyguards said.

The other bodyguards were talking into their earpieces requesting backup.

"Alright hello everyone," Susan said. She was half asleep from the long night she had with little rest. She had to be on top of her game, to be alert not to say something stupid due to exhaustion.

"Alright let's be orderly. We are not girls at a Beatles concert. We are grown adults with jobs. I get that you all have questions, but I cannot hear all of your questions at once. So, let's make this orderly so I can answer more questions," Susan said.

The same yelling stranger cheered, "Yeahhh Suusssaan."

"That guy is too energized it's seven in the morning dude," Susan said.

The crowd laughed.

"Dr. King, do you want to take this outside or somewhere not so cramped?" Her bodyguard whispered something.

"Yep," Susan said.

"Alright if you are a reporter or cameraman, we are going to be taking this outside so let us get through or we will make you let us through! We don't like making people do things," the bodyguard said. The three guards stood up and then helped Susan get out of the booth.

It was chaotic inside the restaurant as a mob of eighty people walked through a tiny door behind Susan King.

"That stage would work," Susan said to her guard. He escorted her quickly onto the stage that was still being assembled.

"Sir, you cannot ..." the worker said.

"We can. Or you can see some iron bars, you decide," the guard said.

The worker chose to let Susan on the stage as he continued to work.

Susan tapped on the microphone and it was really loud. She did not expect it to be on, but it was.

"Shall we begin a few minutes early?" Susan asked.

"Over here, Dr. King. I am live with ABC, and what information do you have regarding the president?" the reporter asked.

John was watching television as he was monitoring the live feed.

"We go live to Andy who is in Nevada where Susan King is speaking," a reporter said.

"Yes Cheryl, Susan King was eating at the restaurant across the street when she moved outside to the stage behind me. She is answering questions ... no she was not scheduled to speak ... let's listen in to what she is saying," Andy said.

"I think that the experiment is moving in a forward direction," Susan said.

"There are allegations that you have stolen money from the government and that your experiment is being investigated, what do you have to say?" a reporter asked.

"I can say that I will not comment. I will add that I have never stolen money and never would, I think that is a horrible thing for someone like myself to do. I would not do anything that puts myself or my experiment at risk because I have spent my life doing this experiment," Susan said.

"What does the president want to do at your experiment?" a reporter asked.

"He wants to see it because he has never seen it in person... I am not sure what else he plans," Susan said.

John was curious how Susan managed to cause such a scene with the reporters. He thought it was Susan being Susan, with her anything could happen.

"I will have to ask her about this one," John said to himself.

He continued to watch the live report. He changed the channel and saw their live report from the small town.

"Breaking news! Susan King is doing a surprise appearance right outside the headquarters of the King's Pawn, where President Devrai is scheduled to be in just a few hours. We have a reporter live at the event," the female reporter said.

"Susan King is answering questions after coming out of that small restaurant. She then walked to this stage where she is talking right now," the reporter at the scene said.

"How do you get through every day, being as tough as it is?" someone asked.

"Wow great question. I have always put the experiment first. Not my life, but more a matter of what does the experiment need. I have pulled all-nighters hundreds of times because the experiment needed me to. The list goes on, but as for what motto I follow, nothing will stop my experiment, nothing! Mark my words," Susan said.

John knew that Susan was not telling the truth because she had stolen money, and she was greedy, and did not always put the experiment first. She had her moments. She did her best to keep them hidden from the public but she did not care about hiding them on a daily basis. He had a gut feeling that something would stop her experiment: her.

Location: California

It was very early in the morning when the president finally woke up. He got ready in the small hotel room. The secret service booked an entire Hilton for just the president. He had the run of the whole place. This Hilton happened to be in downtown Los Angeles.

"Larry what is on schedule for today?" the president asked.

"Yes Mr. President, we are heading to Nevada for the King's Pawn," Larry said.

"Ah yes, I forgot, I'm sorry. I am going to get some breakfast at this buffet," the president said.

"Whatever you wish Mr. President. We will have two guards directly near you, but we have this whole place tied down," Larry said.

"Don't you always have every place tied down?" the president asked sarcastically.

"That's our job sir," Larry said.

The president went down the elevator from the 21st floor to the lobby. The hotel workers were still working as if the hotel was booked out, but the room cleaning staff got a break.

"Hello, how are you?" the president asked the receptionist.

"I am good Mr. President," the lady said. This was the highlight of her short career. It was her first month at the hotel.

"How long have the press been waiting?" the president asked after he noticed the group of media and fans outside.

"They have been here all night Mr. President," she said.

"Sir, we have to get going," one of the secret service members said. There were twenty secret service members in the lobby alone, and another dozen outside. There were about forty throughout the property.

"Let me eat and then we can talk, come join me," the president said to the guard.

"Jonathan, let's talk," Larry said as he stepped off the elevator.

"Alright, care for some tea?" the president asked.

"I am fine, thank you. But I want you to see the news, it's Susan!" Larry said.

The receptionist had heard their conversation and turned the news on for them.

"How?" the president asked.

"She is Susan that's how," Larry said.

"Very true," the president said.

"So, the plan is to get you to the airport and then we will fly in Air Force One to Area 51. We will then drive or fly to that city where you will deliver a surprise speech. Then we will attempt to get you to the experiment with no hitches," Larry said.

"Alright so I will expect to do none of that because what you say is never what happens," the president said.

"Very funny, I am serious this time," Larry said.

"I like the plan," the president said as he glanced at the media again.

"Can you believe they waited all night? We aren't even going out the front door!" the president said.

"It's a security risk, that's why," Larry said.

"Well we aren't going out the front, but that doesn't mean I am not taking a detour out the front door," the president said with a big smile.

"No please ..." Larry did not have time to finish his sentence because the president was already walking out the door.

The president got up and walked right outside as if it were his backyard. He had the tendency to greet the public.

"Hello, the president has left the building," the president said.

At that point a dozen security guards nearly had heart attacks. The president of the United States was in front of a hotel in one of the busiest cities in the country, with no barrier between himself and the people.

"The president is outside, all members," one of the secret service members said into their ear piece. All of the agents began running full speed to the front of the Hilton, Los Angeles street.

"Larry, fetch my ride. Bring it out front," the president said.

"But sir," Larry said.

"But, but, oh ... but you're fired," the president said.

"I will get it here immediately," Larry said.

"That's the spirit!" the president said.

The media and other people were standing outside. There were about a hundred people.

"Down here Mr. President," a lady yelled.

"Over here," another person yelled.

People were also trying to reach their arm out hoping that the president would sign their items. The security that managed to get outside quickly already were trying to prevent the arm reaching.

"Guys calm down. I know what you want to hear so let me say it," the president said.

"Mr. President, what is ..." someone started to say.

"I am going to be at the King's Pawn later today, I am excited and yeah that's what you wanted to hear," the president said.

He then started to walk away from the door towards the crowd.

"I'm signing," the president said to Larry who was standing right next to him.

The president approached the first person and started to sign autographs.

"Thank you so much Mr. President," the person said.

"No problem," the president replied.

"Can I get a selfie?" someone asked.

"Yes," the president said. He did not mind taking photos with people.

As people on the streets started to notice a large crowd, the crowd started to grow.

"Someone give me something cool to sign," the president said.

"Over here! Try this," some random guy yelled. He was holding a baseball.

"Yeah I'll try this," the president said.

"Do you have other people sign baseballs?" the president asked.

"Yep I have everyone sign one I think it's cool," the guy said.

"For sure. All I know is there aren't many of these out there so enjoy. I guess I am cool," the president said.

The autograph came out better than expected because the president signs a very complicated yet quick signature.

"Mr. President one minute more," Larry said.

"Ok, ok," the president replied.

"I have to be going soon guys sorry," the president said to the crowd.

He tried to sign as many autographs as possible in different parts of the crowd. By the end, he started using an abbreviated signature with just his initials J.D.

One person held out a book to get signed. The president never wrote a book.

"Whose book is this?" the president asked as he was signing other items nearby.

"Not sure, I just grabbed one! Can you sign it please?" the guy asked.

"No can do. It's not my book dude! I won't sign it!" the president said.

"Come on Mr. President!" the guy said. The president signed for people standing around the guy.

"Car is around the corner please stop signing," Larry whispered to the president.

"My work here is done. Come to Nevada if you want a second chance for an interview or autograph. Peace out," the president said as he threw up the blue sharpie marker.

"How's that?" the president asked Larry. They looked at the crowd who was very happy to get an interview and a signed item from the same time. Waiting all night does pay off.

"It's splendid. Don't do it again without telling us. We are, well you are lucky we had men out here!" Larry said.

The other secret service members made the crowd move out from under the crescent entrance drive way so the limo could get in.

"My ride's here, folks. It has been a great trip," the president said as the car pulled up, blocking the crowd's view of him.

The crowd started to boo.

Three black SUVs had pulled up and the president would get in one of them. Usually it was the middle one, and it would be for this ride. The secret service members did the same thing on each car, open the door facing away from the crowd so they could not tell which car the president got into.

When the president got into the car he was off to the airport.

"Well now I can relax for a bit," the president said.

"Indeed, but please don't do that again ever!" Larry said.

"I had to give the crowd and news something worth their time to cover. And I thought firing the head honcho would be the perfect way to get people talking. You are not actually fired I hope you caught on," the president said.

"I played along," Larry said.

"Good times good times," the president said.

About thirty minutes later the motorcade was approaching LAX.

"I miss being able to live here like a regular person," the president said.

"It is tough I can imagine," Larry said.

His phone started to ring.

"No ... that is not okay ... we are talking the president not a celebrity. We will leave at the original time no matter what ... a fire won't stop the president," Larry said into his phone.

"What's wrong?" the president asked.

"There was a fire that shut the runways down for a bit so they are delayed ... they said we were too, but I denied that," Larry said.

"We are early, aren't we?" the president asked.

"Yes, and if we arrive early then they should be ready based on the coverage Susan's special appearance got," Larry said.

"How early are we right now?" the president asked.

"Over two hours," Larry said.

"Well it's only two hours, I mean two hours cannot hurt, unless they have something to hide," the president said.

"You are too funny Mr. President. Our first hurdle is getting to the plane," Larry said.

"Wait I want to make a video for my YouTube channel. I want to prove to them that this experiment is legit!" the president said.

"And if it is not legit?" Larry asked.

"Then we do not upload the video ... well then, the guys in charge of my YouTube channel won't upload the video," the president said.

"That can be our cover to get evidence if we need to," the driver said.

"Yes, that sounds like a good idea, tell that to the rest of our clan," Larry said.

Getting to the plane turned out to be easier than expected for the president. Their only problem was the fifteen other planes waiting in line to takeoff.

The president was sitting in his mobile office unaware of the obstacles the pilots were facing.

"Air Force One to command, do you read me?" the head pilot asked.

"Command to Air Force One, affirmative," the air traffic control member said.

"Air Force One requesting permission to taxi to runway."

"Command to Air Force One, access denied."

"Again, Air Force One requesting access to take off. We have the president on board we must take off."

"There are no available runways."

"Then we will taxi around them all."

"It is dangerous, give us ten minutes. Do not taxi."

"We are taking off regardless! Hold all other departures until we are in the sky over and out."

"Command to Air Force One, there is no clearance."

The plane was parked away from the other airlines. The plane had begun to taxi during the conversation, but there were not any available runways. The only runway was the main one or a smaller one for private jets.

"Air Force One to command, requesting permission to take off from runway A3 … again A3."

"Access granted. Head to A3."

Runway A3 was a much smaller runway, but the pilots knew what they could and could not do with the plane. They had experience taking off from the most dangerous runways in the world, so the small runway was no challenge.

"Attention passengers, Mr. President, we have been granted access to takeoff from a smaller runway. This may be bumpy," the pilot said over the speaker.

They first had to get to the runway.

"Air Force One to Delta flight 81872, please hold again please cease all procedures of takeoff," the pilot said.

"Delta flight 81872 to Air Force One, we read you loud and clear," the delta pilot said as he turned his plane off the runway.

Many people in airplanes and in waiting gates saw the famous blue and white airplane with the United States emblem on the side. They were surprised to see the plane taxiing around the other planes. They were lining up on the main runway nearly causing a collision with two other airplanes who had begun to move.

"Command to AF1 stop immediately!"

"AF1 to command thank you for your service to us. We are done here."

The huge airplane had begun the takeoff procedure of gaining speed.

"Mr. President we are taking off from the main runway," the pilot said over the speaker.

"Great," the president said, even though nobody heard him.

Location – 30,000 feet high. 40 miles out from Area 51

"So here is your speech," Larry said to the president. The two men were sitting in a conference room alone talking about the game plan and schedule.

"Alright," the president said.

"What is the plan?" he continued.

"We land at Area 51 and get you to the experiment by helicopter. The cars will be waiting for you at the experiment because afterwards you will be driven into the town for your speech," Larry said.

"I am sure there is more to this than you are telling me," the president said.

"Oh yes there is a lot, but it is the norm for you. Things like meeting the soldiers when you get off the plane, being followed by the press," Larry said.

"That's what I wanted to hear. Why Area 51 though?" the president asked.

"It is the closest secure airport to the experiment that we can land this plane in. The key is landing. And it is secure, so we will not have any press stopping us. And the helicopters are already there," Larry said.

"About this speech ... none of it is true," the president said after he read the speech that he did not write.

"Your job is to make it seem true, that's what you do best," Larry said.

"Yes, but I do not like lying to the American people," the president said.

Someone knocked on the door.

"Sorry to interrupt you Mr. President, I have a call for you right here," a man in a suit said.

The man handed the president the phone.

"Jonathan Devrai speaking," the president said.

"Mr. President, I am the mayor of New York, there has been an attack here at Wall Street," the mayor said.

"You have got to be kidding me!" the president said. "This could not have been a worse time!"

"The media is all over the place, I just wanted to let you know," the mayor said.

"Thank you, I will handle whatever I need to," the president said. He then hung up on the mayor.

"Looks like our battle ship has been hit again," the president said.

"Where at?" Larry asked.

"Wall Street," the president said.

"That's terrible! That's where the New York Stock Exchange is!" Larry said.

"I know! Strategic on their end...," the president said.

"What do you plan to do?" Larry asked.

"I plan to do my job, see the experiment and I will address the attack in the speech so someone has some work to do," the president said.

"I will get that done immediately," Larry said.

"First we have a rodeo to attend. Shall we?" the president asked.

"Yes," Larry said.

Location- Headquarters

Susan was in her office after dealing with the press. The phone started ringing.

"Susan King ... who am I speaking to?"

"You are speaking with Larry with the United States Secret Service."

"Alright ..."

"So, we have landed at a secure area and we are going to be flying via helicopter to your location. Where can we land the Presidential helicopters?"

"How many helicopters are you talking about?"

"Three helicopters."

"Alright ... I hope you realize that we are in the middle of a dessert, there's plenty of places to land your helicopters. Just be careful of the buildings."

"It is estimated we will arrive by 10:38."

"That's three hours early!"

"Yes it is; at the request of the president we left early."

"The president requests no press or media and full access to the society."

"Larry, tell her I want into the society," the president said from the background.

"I cannot make any promises, the experiment is very delicate," Susan said.

"Just to let you know Dr. King, we have fifteen secret service agents with us. They go where the president goes."

"There are already ten agents here securing our already secure area," Susan said. Nobody responded and ten seconds later Susan realized that Larry hung up on her.

"Commander!" Susan yelled from her office.

The Commander came to her office to see what she wanted.

"The president will be here in less than an hour!" Susan said.

"They were not supposed to get here until noon!" Commander said.

"I want a full staff briefing here in five minutes. They don't all have to be here, but I want everyone to hear the briefing," Susan said.

Five minutes later, Susan started to give the briefing to the small army of her closest aides.

"So, the president will be here really soon! Keep everything as perfect as possible. I do not want you to talk to him unless he talks to you. Under no circumstances will Jonathan Devrai get into the society. If anyone asks you questions do not answer them... no matter what they say. I cannot afford for my crimes to be discovered by them, and I think they will try to search for my crimes. Are there any questions?" Susan asked.

"Yes Susan, what can they do to us anyways?" someone asked.

"They can shut us down and arrest me for tax evasion, and for stealing money from the government," Susan said.

"And that would cause for us to be shut down," John finished.

"Let's make this day successful," Susan said.

John and Derek were watching the news when they saw the breaking news.

"Breaking news out of New York. Just moments ago, the New York Stock Exchange was attacked by terrorists. An eyewitness at the scene said five men with guns shot aimlessly inside. As of right now over one hundred and three people have been confirmed dead, but that number is due to increase. The president issued a statement 'America is falling on hard times right now! My condolences to the victims and their families. We cannot let this happen again.' We will get back to you when we get more details," the reporter said.

"Now on a more pleasant note, President Devrai is currently flying from Los Angeles to Nevada where he will meet with Susan King and see the experiment first hand. The president was staying at the Hilton downtown when he surprised media and fans by walking outside ... see for yourself," the same reporter said.

"I am going to be at the King's Pawn later today, I am excited and yeah that's what you wanted to hear," the president said to the reporters.

"The president did our job for us. From New York, you are watching Good Morning Everyone," the reporter finished.

"Susan!" John yelled.

"Yes, John what do you need?" Susan yelled back.

"Come here please," he yelled.

"Alright," she replied in a conversational tone, but John could not hear her response.

"I just saw this on the news," John said.

He replayed the news for Susan to see just moments after it aired.

"Oh my god!" Susan said.

"It's terrible," Derek said joining in on the conversation.

"The president is being hammered by all of these vicious attacks," John said.

"It shows you how terrible this world is," Susan said.

"This is like the second attack this week!" Derek said.

"What was the other one?" Susan asked.

"The school. That's why the president was in Los Angeles to begin with," John said.

"Maybe you should acknowledge the attacks in your speech Susan," Derek recommended.

"Why would I do that?" Susan asked.

"Well it would show that you care about other people and not yourself because people think you are selfish," Derek said.

"How could you ..." Susan exclaimed.

"I do not think you are selfish, but the news and media do, I'm just telling you what's out there," Derek said.

"He's right," John said.

"Well I will definitely add that to the speech," Susan said.

"Guys, go put suits on, in case I bring you with me," Susan said.

"Yes ma'am," the two said. They went to the bedroom to grab their suits to change into.

Susan walked back to her office to revise her speech.

"Wow that is a great idea; why did I not think to mention the current events long ago," she mumbled to herself.

A few minutes later, John again called Susan to his office via the intercom.

"What now?" Susan said.

"Look," John said. He pulled up the live camera showing the entrance to the experiment property. The entrance that goes to the real world not the entrance into the society.

"There is a crowd out there!" Susan exclaimed.

"That's why I called you ... how do they know exactly where this is?" John asked.

"There's no way! We are like thirty miles out into the middle of a desert literally!" Susan said.

"We will have to tighten security there and make sure the president lands away from their view," Susan said.

"Derek please tell Commander to position ten more guards near the fence," Susan said. "We could use the extra protection just in case."

"I will do that immediately," Derek said.

"More importantly how do they know exactly where we are?" Susan asked.

"I have no clue," John said.

"Let's just hope they don't mention our location," Derek said.

"Someone must have told them," Susan said.

Chapter Twenty-Three

The President, Jonathan Devrai was on his way to see the King's Pawn experiment. His plane, Air Force One landed at Area 51, a top secret military base.

"Wow I love Area 51!" the president said.

"It is interesting," Larry said.

"The only bad part is nobody on earth but the people who work here and us know what really goes on here," the president said.

"It is a matter of national security," Larry said.

"I know, but I do not like the fact that Americans have been lied to for more than half a century!" the president said.

"Well if you want Americans to have a massive alien freak out then be my guest to tell them," Larry said.

"Oh common! What's a little freak out," the president said.

"Statistically speaking a 'little' freak out would cause an unprecedented retaliation against the government," Larry said.

"Because we hid this from them for years ... I don't blame the people, I would retaliate with them," the president said.

"The longer the public does not know what goes on here, the longer they stay safe," Larry said.

"I think it is funny how so many Americans have tried to get into Area 51 through the front door. I mean we aren't inviting them in the front door! At least use the side door, c'mon America! Even I know not to break in through the front door" the president said jokingly.

"They truly have tried everything," Larry said.

"I remember when that one really, really smart guy thought it would be smart to attempt to parachute into Area 51 from a plane. The joke was on him because he completely missed the fact that this is a no fly zone," the president said.

"Oh yeah! I remember that too. That brilliant, brilliant man is now in jail," Larry said.

"Well I have to give him credit, nobody else tried it but he overlooked the reasoning behind it. He totally overlooked how he would get in the air," the president said.

"What a moron," Larry said. The two men laughed.

"What the people do not know is that Area 51 is one of our weaker locations. Once they get past the first line of security they are basically inside, because there is not a lot of internal security because nobody has ever passed the front line," the president said.

"Let's keep it that way," Larry said.

"You look stressed," Larry said. He worked with the president long enough to figure out his emotions just by looking at his face.

"I am stressed. I don't know what to do, because I am worried about these recent attacks. They are becoming a common occurrence and that reflects me as a president."

"Attacks are on the rise according to stats," Larry said to back up what the president just said.

"I get that! I am playing the role of the firemen always fighting the fire, never preventing the fire before it happens," the president said. Clearly, he was a bit frustrated.

"I agree with you," Larry said.

"What we need to do is tighten security and not let these attacks get publicity because that's what these people want is to cause a change. We need to prevent the fires!" the president said.

"Attention ladies and gentlemen, we are landing in five minutes," the pilot said over the speaker.

"So, Mr. President, we are going to get you off this plane and onto your helicopter. The first one," Larry said.

"Sounds good," the president said.

"I want this all to go smoothly. No mistakes, there will be tons of people, most of them media. That means there is a lot of variables," the president continued.

"I will brief the team when we get airborne again, but I think this will be alright," Larry said.

"Sorry for the interruption of our conversation sir," Larry said.

"No need to apologize," the president said.

Air Force One landed with no problems. The president made an effort to greet every person on the tarmac who came out to see the airplane land. It took the president nearly fifteen minutes to get into the helicopter. The plan was only two minutes maximum.

"Hello Mr. President," a soldier said.

"Hello sir, thank you for your service," the president said as he gave a salute followed by a handshake, before running up the steps and into the helicopter. He was known for being a down to earth man.

The interior of the helicopter was different from the others, the exterior was the exact same. The president had the interior gutted and rebuilt with larger seats and more technology. The tough part was keeping it as safe as the others in the fleet if not even safer.

"Mr. President, it will be about a thirty minute flight," Larry said.

"Sounds perfect," the president said.

"I have my speech here on my phone. I do want it on paper if at all possible," the president said.

"You will have two teleprompters," Larry said.

"That's much better actually, less chance of a technical breakdown," the president said.

The helicopter took off in one fluid motion. It was much different than the airplane.

When the fleet was airborne, Larry got a call to his phone.

"Hello Dr. King," Larry said.

"Do not fly over my society with your helicopter!" Susan said.

"Alright we will try our best," Larry said.

"No! Not your best! You will not fly over, there's no option," Susan said.

"We do what we need to get the president safely on the ground. Goodbye," Larry said as he hung up on Susan yet again.

"These idiots! They keep hanging up on me!" Susan said angrily in her office.

Location - Society

I was driving a rac when I heard the deep rumbling noise. It was like no other, it was uneven. It was also very abrupt, like a large gathering of people speaking all at once.

I first heard the noise then saw the objects. There were three of them, which was literally an odd amount. They were not square or even rounded, but rather a new shape. They had a long thin back and very tiny wheels. There were three circles, one on each of the flying objects. I had never seen anything like them before and I immediately wondered what they were.

Location - Headquarters

"Dr. King you may want to see this quickly, like really quickly!" John said. Susan came running into his office.

"What in the ..." Susan said.

"Helicopters! Three of them," John said.

"I know what helicopters look like!" Susan said angrily before swearing.

"And they are over society," Derek said.

"I just got off the phone with them! I told them fly around my society," Susan said. "I told them that hell will be unleashed if they don't obey my order!"

"Well they didn't listen," John said emphasizing they.

"And they will be in big trouble. We will release hell," Susan said. She too emphasized the word they.

"What do you want to do about this?" Derek asked.

"I have a very good plan. If he won't listen to my orders I won't listen to his. Exactly twenty minutes after the president arrives I want a code red. That will get him out and give us a valid reason to get him out," Susan said.

"Are you crazy?" Derek asked.

"Very," Susan said.

"So, you want a fake code red?" John asked.

"So, I suppose," Susan said.

"But who will issue it?" Derek asked.

"You will," Susan replied.

"Remember twenty minutes! Set a timer if you must," Susan said as she walked out. "The less he sees the better."

"She is crazy!" John said under his breath, loud enough so his coworker could hear him.

"I think she is a little angry about the whole flying over the society thing," Derek said.

"I think you're right, but let's not make her any more angry," Derek continued.

They could hear her yelling and swearing in anger.

"Well, Mount St. Helens just blew its top again!" John said.

Derek laughed.

The news reporters standing outside the entrance to the government property knew when the president arrived, they heard it. They all scrambled to get the best shot of the sound and report the event. Some were even so desperate as to attempt to fly drones over the wall. The drones never made it back over the wall. Derek saw the drones fall out of the sky on the cameras. Susan had a GPS and WiFi jammer installed so any technology would be fried if it came over the wall. The technology below the wall was safe.

All of the reporters were talking at the same time, causing a scene.

The president saw the society from the sky and he was amazed. He was the reason the helicopters flew over the society. He noted the perfection and symmetry of the society.

Susan King had made a valiant effort to personally greet the president. She brought the Commander with her.

"Hello Dr. King," the president said reaching out his hand to shake Susan's.

"Hello Mr. President," Susan replied. "Long time no see."

Both Susan and the president laughed at this comical comment.

"Ha, ha, it has been quite some time," the president said.

"It's very nice to be here. Shall we get inside, it's rather hot out here," the president said.

He followed Susan to the headquarters which was a very short stroll away.

"So how long did this take to construct?" the president asked as the clan of people walked towards the front door of the building,

"Well this, our headquarters took a few years and went slightly over budget. The experiment has taken 15 years so far," Susan said.

"That's a really long time!" the president said.

"Yes it is, not including the years it took me to get this whole thing started. That alone was a huge undertaking," Susan said.

They all walked into the lobby of the headquarters which was desolate. One person greeted them at the door.

"This is the Commander," Susan said.

"Hello Mr. President. My name is Adrian Commelson. Call me Commander. It is an honor to meet you," Commander said. He was very excited to meet the president.

"Nice to meet you too," the president replied.

The clan entered the headquarters and went to the top floor. They were crammed in the small elevator, most of the people were secret service agents.

"This is where everything is monitored, assessed and even changed," Susan said as the elevator door opened up to the large room.

"Looks like NASA in here," the president said.

"Well this basically is NASA, these people work tough jobs but without them my experiment would have failed 15 years ago," Susan said.

Susan saw the president eyeing the large screens.

"So, the screens you are seeing are two things. The first is top secret, classified and the second is they are inside the society hidden," Susan said.

"How do the people not see cameras?" the president asked.

"Again Mr. President they are very hidden, and they are entirely custom so the cameras you are picturing look nothing like mine," Susan said.

"Mr. President, this is one of the cameras," the Commander said. He handed the president a small circular object that was about the size of a pen.

"Wow it's so small! Not even the white house has cameras like these," the president said.

Susan smiled and said, "Nobody has cameras like these. They are custom made and they were not cheap either."

"I could imagine! But you could stick these puppies anywhere and with some cords, bam, you have workin' cameras that nobody would ever spot," the president said.

"Well we would need thousands of miles of cords. These are wireless and work on their own individual network that we connect to," Susan said.

"You think of everything," the president said.

"Well I did not think of these," Susan said.

"I did," the Commander said to restate that he thought of the idea, not Susan.

"Well ... after the experiment sell these to make some extra money, but do not forget your patent," the president said.

"Oh I have no intentions of selling the idea," Susan said. As she put thought into the idea, she really liked the idea of selling the cameras, but she would choose not to sell them.

"Let me give you a virtual tour," Susan said a few minutes later. The president walked around the headquarters and really loved her office, fit for any king. He also spoke briefly with John and Derek.

"Huh, I was not really thinking virtual tour. I was thinking of an actual tour in person," the president said.

"I am afraid I cannot do that Mr. President. I cannot even go inside the experiment and I created the thing," Susan said.

This response confused the president because what she said made no sense to him. "Why is that?" he asked.

"Well do not forget the fact that this is a live experiment, with extremely fine-tuned variables. Life inside is quite literally perfect, and we are considered imperfect to them. They would notice my hair color for example is more than one color. Your security with guns would be a huge problem," Susan said.

The president nodded in agreement before he replied, "I guess that makes sense but please I really want to go inside. Just me and you."

"Susan, we have a problem!" Derek said over the loudspeaker. Susan realized that the twenty minutes had past, but she was lost in time.

"Mr. President, please excuse me as something has come up ... it happens ... sometimes, well actually it happens a lot," Susan said.

"But my ..." the president said. He was disappointed because he was looking forward to the tour.

"Your tour will wait," Susan said firmly over her shoulder as she ran to Derek. She wanted to make the situation look as real as possible.

The president had no clue what to do as everyone scattered to their positions much like naval officers on a battleship during combat.

Susan walked into Derek and John's office and shut the door. Her posture changed completely.

"Alright let's do this," she said.

"Here is the microphone," John said as he handed Susan a pencil. Susan decided to make the microphone a pencil as a prank for the two men. Especially when they had multiple pencils, if they grabbed the wrong one it would project their voices.

"I am issuing a code red! Again, I repeat a code red status right now ... please monitor," Susan said into her pencil microphone as she smiled.

The president was still in the headquarters taking a good look around the main room at all of the televisions and people conducting their work in an office setting. He was surprised that an experiment was being run like a surveillance center.

"What's going on?" he asked Larry.

"Sir I have no clue, it doesn't sound good," Larry said.

"Send someone to find out ... Susan is in that room," the president said as he pointed to the office.

"Yes sir," Larry said.

"Agent Bradford please go to the office for John and Derek. Ask Dr. King what is happening and what we should do," Larry said into his earpiece.

"Yes sir," Agent Bradford replied.

There was a knock on the door.

"It's an agent," Derek said. All he had to do was look at the wall, specifically at the camera positioned outside the door.

Susan went to open the door grudgingly.

"Hello! What can I do for you on this fine totally not busy morning?" Susan asked sarcastically.

"The president is requesting information. He wants to know what is happening and what would be the best thing for him to do at this time?" Agent Bradford asked.

Susan motioned for the agent to make himself comfortable

"Please come in take a seat," Susan said.

"Dr. King we do not have time to fool around," Agent Bradford said.

"So basically, we have codes depending on the situation. We do not want them, they are bad! Code red is the worst, meaning something is very wrong. It is at these times when I have to best address the situation at hand," Susan said, purposely treating the Agent like a young child.

"What should the president do?" Agent Bradford asked.

"He should get you out of this room as soon as possible and let me continue to do my job. More reasonably, he can stay here or go to the town. Whatever works for you, because *you* are of the utmost importance to me right now. If *you* and your party chose to leave I will join you when this is sorted out. You tell me," Susan said with a very obvious disrespectful attitude towards the Agent. She had a very rude emphasis on the word "you" almost an insulting tone.

"I will advise the president and find out what he prefers. My apologies for my interruption Dr. King," Agent Bradford said.

"Apology accepted. Bye-bye now!" Susan said.

The agent closed the door to the office as he left. He muttered under his breath "what a rude woman!"

"Now that he is gone we wait and pretend," Susan said.

The staff were reflecting on how Susan acted, but nobody felt like confronting her about it until Derek spoke for the others. "Why did you treat him like that?" he asked.

"Listen, if I treated everyone nicely then I would not be here because people take advantage of others. It just so happens that the follower doesn't come out victorious in the real world. I will not be the follower," Susan said. "After all, it's a part of the business."

"Are you saying it is okay to deceive people?" John asked.

"Yes, because if you don't then they will deceive you! If I didn't take chances then we would not be here with the president of the United States!" Susan exclaimed.

"Mr. President, Dr. King said that we could stay on premises or move into the city. The choice is yours," Agent Bradford said.

The president replied quickly, "I think we move ... why not?"

"Mr. President, you told me that you wanted Susan with you on stage, has your wish changed?" Larry asked just to make sure he did not make a mistake.

"Nope, but we may be a hindrance to these people who are doing a very tough job. On the other hand, let's wait a few minutes," the president said.

"The boy needs to rise up the chain. I don't want to wait too long. This experiment is too slow, like let's speed this up a bit," Susan said impatiently. Her desire for everything to be done quickly was first noticed by Derek, who learned to sense Susan's emotions.

"Well in my opinion we should be very careful not to mess up anything dramatic. For example, you cannot change the leader overnight, it would confuse the society, alter the meticulous data, and end our experiment," he said.

"Oh darn! I was literally thinking overnight," Susan said with noticeable anticipation.

"Susan, I am currently listening to the conversation between the president and that agent, they don't plan on going anywhere anytime soon," John said. He had headphones on and was listening to the audio from the camera outside his office. Truly everything was under a watchful eye.

"That's fine I guess," Susan said.

"But what should we do about the Chief Elder? It's been a long time ..." Derek asked.

"I have some plans," Susan said.

Chapter Twenty-Four

Over time, things became more predictable in a way. As each day worked the same for members of society, each day worked differently for me. As time passed, experiences and unexpected events also passed.

I had taken a notice to the actions of the Chief Elder. He was aged much more than any other society member. His actions were much slower, but his ability to think had never slowed, and his personality never slowed.

I was well practiced in the art of decisions. I was able to make tough choices, but only in practice with the device. I had never made a choice that would affect the members of society, and I did not think I would ever need to.

I vividly recall the one day that changed the society.

It was early in the day ... the light was up in the sky, there were white objects in the sky also. I went down the stairs for some food, but something had changed, there was no aroma of food. I went to go look for the Chief Elder because he was not preparing our meal like he did every day. That was a bit odd, but maybe he forgot to wake up, so I first checked to see if he was in his room. He was not, so I searched around the home, every section ... and I still could not find him. I looked everywhere I could think to look.

"Hello, sir?" I called out as I was walking around looking. "Can you hear me?"

There was no response.

I was very puzzled because I did not know what to do. I went to the room where I used the device, anticipating to find a schedule or some more information.

There was nothing there ... that was not usually there.

I decided to go to the building I first met the Chief Elder at, hoping he would be there. I used the rac that the Chief Elder used. That was one sign, he would have used his car to travel anywhere. With this in mind I still figured to look elsewhere.

As I was moving through society, I noticed the same things, nothing out of ordinary, life was normal for everyone else.

In our society when one passes, a loud bell is rung two times. It could be heard anywhere in our society, no matter your location. It is a very noticeable sound due to how loud it was. In addition, it was rare for a society member to pass, as it happened only a few times over my life.

I was on the way to the building when I heard four loud bells. Four bells are for one of the heads of society. At that time I connected the two things together, a missing Elder and four bells.

I was the Chief Elder, the youngest one in our Society. I was not aged enough to be an elder, I was only a youth. I had no clue what to do. I continued on my original route, until I heard a voice out of nowhere.

"You can hear me, I know you can," a voice said firmly.

I was a bit puzzled as to why this voice was speaking to me. "Who are you? Where am I hearing you from?" I asked hoping to answer my own question.

"I am projecting my voice through your rac," the voice replied ignoring my question.

"Okay then," I said.

"The Chief Elder is dead ... passed," the voice said.

I was confused when I replied, "That means I am the Chief Elder."

"Drive to the Condemning Station, where you will be advised. You are the Chief Elder," the voice said.

"Why?" I asked.

There was no response, so I did as I was told by the voice.

I arrived at the Condemning Station to be greeted by the same member who took my sister in. She was wearing the same attire as in the past. Nothing had changed about her.

"We are expecting your arrival," she said emotionless.

"Ok, I was told to come here," I said.

"Please follow me right this way," she said. She got up out of her seat in one fluid motion.

She led me to a new area, one I had never seen. There was a door, the signage on the door read "Private." She knocked two times.

After waiting a few moments, she said to me, "Please enter."

I opened the door and I was facing the head members of society. The room itself was different, the table was some sort of curve shape. Almost like a football from sports, but a flat version.

There were twelve members and an empty seat at the end of the table. My seat was respectively at the head of the table representing that I was the head of society.

"Welcome," one of the members said.

"Greetings," I said.

"Please sit," someone else said.

After I sat down I realized that I was in a very important meeting.

"Our head of society, has passed. This young youth is now the Chief Elder," the elder to my right said.

I viewed my position as humorously ironic, I was very young, yet my position deemed me an elder.

"I am the Succeeding Elder. My position is your advisor, and I assist you in times of request. I want you to be reminded that the society rests on your choices," he said.

"Thank you, I understand my powers," I said.

"You will have the ability to change any part of the code. Your choice is always final, as we cannot override your choice. You have the ability to override our choices," the Succeeding Elder said.

"How do I change the code?"

"You write the change and give it to us and we have the scribesmen add it to the code," he said.

Another elder started talking. "It will be your responsibility to rule over and make a verdict on any rebellious character. As you should be aware, the highest reprimand is banishment or unnatural passing," the elder said.

My mental state changed a lot during the meeting. I felt overwhelmed, almost to the point where I felt as if I could not suppress my emotions.

"You have the power to change the lives of members of society, what you do is up to you," another elder said.

Another elder started to speak just as the previous sentence was completed. "Society does not know of this yet, we want a smooth transition of power," they said.

"I am requesting permission to excuse myself please," I said.

"Granted," the 12 elders said in harmony. I never knew how they were able to speak in perfect harmony, comes with practice I thought.

I wanted to talk to my parents, because I really did not know what to do with my power or situation. I had practiced with the Chief Elder in the room with the device, but I had never made decisions for others, only simulated situations which never truly represented our situation accurately.

I went back to the rac and drove to my home. The sights were very familiar. The same homes in the same place with the same grass, everything was the same, it was just a cycle of similarity.

When I arrived at my home, I noticed that our families rac was on the property. I stationed my new, larger rac next to the white one, and went to the door, which presumably would be unlocked.

As expected, the door was not locked, due to The Code. I quietly entered and my mother was sitting in a chair reading a book.

"Hello mother," I said.

"Hello honey," she said loudly, as she jumped. She was startled by my unexpected appearance in the middle of the day.

"Aren't you supposed to be at your occupation today?" I asked. I still did not know what her occupation was, but I really did not care given the situation at hand.

"No, I have an extra gifted day," she said.

"Aren't you supposed to be with the Chief Elder honey?" She asked.

"That's why I came to see you. Nobody but myself and some Elders know about my situation," I said.

"What's wrong?" She asked.

"I … I am the Chief Elder," I said stuttering my way through the sentence.

"How! Wait what!?" She said very emotionally. Her reaction did not seem real, but more like a reaction of someone who already knew the fact.

"The Chief Elder passed earlier today or in the night," I said.

She did not respond. She knew that an accident must have happened, because she had not been told of such a scenario.

"I was driving to go look where I first met the Chief Elder when a voice told me to go to the Condemning Station. When I arrived, I was directed to a room where some of the head elders were. They told me I am the Chief Elder and what I do or change, impacts all society members," I said.

"Wow, alright let's think this through," she responded.

She sat at the table that was right behind her. I sat down next to her so we were face-to-face.

"When you make decisions, they will now be impacting us and the society. So, when you make choices think to yourself 'how will this impact my family' because you can be more calm then," she said.

"That is a good plan," I said.

"Stay at a calm state of mind, don't let emotions get to your head," she said.

"I can try not to, but it will not be easy," I said.

I realized that I had never been an emotional person, no member of society was.

"This is the first occasion I have felt worried and stressed," I said.

"Well honey, you have never had to face such challenges. Come the passage of time, you will become experienced and accustomed to such challenges," she said.

My mother never failed to calm my emotions when I needed her to.

"What do you think I should change first that will be a positive improvement in our society?" I asked.

"Honey, change what is in need of being changed. You are in the position with rare power to change ideas and rules to benefit the rest of society. You are the members voice, and your own too," she said in an empowering tone.

"Mother, it is not an easy task, as all aspects of society are so organized. There are not many, or any ideas or concepts in need of change," I said.

"Well once you get used to your new position, then you should start making changes, not necessarily at this time," she replied.

She gave me a hug, which was a rare symbolism of love as she said, "I love you honey."

"I love you too mom." It was true, I felt a deep love for my family.

After she hugged me I left and returned to my new home. That trip was very lonely without the Chief Elder being present. It seemed lonely not having another member with me in the rac that was designed to carry a few members of society. Sitting in that silence was overwhelming, that silence seemed to hit me the hardest.

When I got to the home, it was very empty in likeness, and still the silence continued.

I knew that there would be a ceremony regarding the change in power, I did not know when it would be.

I spent the whole day waiting for any more information about the ceremony. I sat and gathered my thoughts about changing The Code and improving the Society. I walked around the large home and ventured into new rooms and the lower level, of which I have never been, just so I could try to think of some ideas.

I happened to be in a deep thought, sitting on the seat of the piano when the telecom rang. I had to hustle over to the counter which was in the adjacent room.

I picked up the phone and asked, "Who am I speaking to?"

"Greetings master, the ceremony will begin at eight hours of the morning, four before noon," the person said. They hung up.

"Well that was quick," I said aloud for no apparent reason.

I had written on the wall one new idea, "Expansion."

I wanted to address the society all at one time, so I wrote a speech for the next day.

The Next Day

I woke up very early and prepared the same meal that the Chief Elder prepared every morning. It felt mostly the same, just without his friendly presence. It was 6:30 when I left the home to get to the location.

In our society, there was a big common area that was very beautiful, it was the heart of society based on location. The Chief Elder deemed that location for ceremonies, and I had no intentions on changing it. For members of society, any and all ceremonies were mandatory to attend.

I drove the blue rac to the center of society. I had my speech and I was prepared to face the entire society.

The drive was very different. I was feeling a lot of stress and I was nervous. I felt the most overwhelmed during these two days. They were tough because the change was so quick, and it was a busy time full of confusion. I had fair reason to be nervous as my entire life changed with no notice.

When I arrived, I had to position the rac before I got out. There was a platform that was set up for me to deliver my speech, so I decided to position the rac directly behind the platform. A crowd was already gathering by 7:16.

Before I got out of the car, the voice started to speak to me again.

"The society does not know of the passing of the Chief Elder. I have arranged a video to explain the process to them," the voice said.

"I was under the guise that the society has been notified of the passing," I said to the voice in the rac.

"Not directly, some may have made the correlation from the four bells, but most have not. All they were told is there is a mandatory ceremony," the voice said.

"Who are you?" I asked.

"You will find out soon enough," the voice said. Again, the voice did not speak again. I wondered if it was the same lady: Susan.

I exited the rac and saw some members of society. The weather was fair, given the time of day. I had so many things on my mind, especially the big speech. It seemed to loom over my head like an umbrella.

"Excuse me Master," a voice said. I looked and realized it was a member of society.

"Hello, can I assist you?" I asked. I realized I had to act like the Chief Elders assistant.

"Yes, I am going to be introducing the ceremony. There will be a video telling society about the ceremony. Afterwards I will call upon you to do your speech, and afterwards you will be sworn in as the Chief Elder. My occupation is the Lead Ceremonial Director," she said. I do not remember what she looked like.

"Thank you. Should I greet people? What do I do?" I asked.

"Master, you can act as you please," she said.

"I will wait," I said.

She then walked away calmly.

I decided to wait on the platform and watch the members arrive. I did not realize how many members there were in our society until I saw all of the seats laid out. Rows upon rows of white symmetrical seats, evenly spaced, like a grid. The chair on the platform, the one I was sitting in, was larger than the ones facing me, but it was still crafted with perfection. The lawn was very green and vibrant, despite the moderately warm temperature.

During this time of waiting, I was just thinking about my situation and trying to hold my emotions back. It was evident that the other members did not have the same emotions that I did, I would try to change that.

As more and more families arrived, I felt more emotions. I recognized some members from education, but I also did not recognize the majority. I saw my sister arrive with my mother and father. I had to go greet them, because I had not seen my sister in a very long time.

My mother saw me first.

"Hi mother!" I said.

"Hi honey, I wish you the best of luck today," she said. My father came up to me from directly behind my mom.

"Hello son, how is your occupation?" my father asked.

"It is very busy. A lot of things are happening all at once," I said.

"I know honey," my mother said.

"How is your occupation?" I asked my sister in hopes to help change the topic to a less stressful one.

"We are getting the first passed member later today or tomorrow," she said.

"Wow that will be a good experience. Just do what you have been taught and everything will go just fine," I said. She smiled but did not reply.

After a short time of silence between us, my sister decided to break it.

"Do you know what this ceremony will be for?" she asked.

I knew the reason, but I did not know if my mother had told her, so I decided it would be the best for her if I did not tell her the real truth.

"I may have a hint, but I do not know if my source is reliable," I said.

"Honey can I talk with you?" my mom asked me.

"Of course, mom," I said.

"Go grab some seats please," she said to my father. He did as she asked of him.

She took me behind the platform where I had positioned my rac.

"Look honey I know this is difficult, very, very difficult! You are doing a great job," she said.

"I am trying my best to not have a mental breakdown," I said. "Plus, there is so much happening in the tiniest time frame."

"I know honey, it is so difficult! But I want you to know something, it's a secret between the two of us," she said. Her tone of voice changed from a regular tone to a very weak whisper.

"I am not supposed to keep secrets, but I will," I said.

"You may think this is an accident, but it is not! From the time when you were a baby, your fate had been predetermined. You have the power to change things, but all of this was meant to happen. I want you to know that you could not have prevented this, it was your destiny. Just do what you think is best," she said.

I thought through what she had just said for a few seconds before I replied. I could not understand what my mom was referring to.

"What do you mean the Chief Elder was meant to pass this early?" I asked.

"Well I have told you too much. Possibly you are right," she said as she turned and went back to find my sister and father.

I went and sat on stage and waited for my time. The clock was ticking down until the society would know my secret, I was the Chief Elder.

I did not realize that I had lost track of time. The time had already come to reveal the secret.

"Welcome Members of this great society! We have gathered today to celebrate a major change in our short history. We have a video prepared to overview our history and the rare occurrence that has happened," the lady said. She was the member I had talked to before the ceremony.

"Over the last many years, we have achieved many great things! We have been the leading society in medical, ecological, and mathematical research! Together we have made the society a better place. Our society started over one hundred years ago. We had one structure, and over one hundred years later, we have over four hundred structures," the narrator said.

A woman's face came on the screen. It was a woman I had seen before somewhere, as I vaguely remembered her. Her hair color was not normal, but rather a mix of a few hues of a color.

"Hello! My name is Susan. I have overseen society for many years, making sure every day works like clockwork. There are many other members of society who have made a change for the good. We have had a Chief Elder who kept society from failing, for the last 15 years … Today marks a new evolution for society. A horrific incident occurred yesterday, the passing of the Chief Elder," Susan said with varying emotion, that most members of society had never witnessed before.

The crowd gasped loudly.

"With the passing of the Chief Elder, comes a ceremony for his young successor. I now introduce to you the youngest Chief Elder in our history," Susan continued.

I knew I had seen Susan somewhere, and the name reminded me of what happened at the Occupation Ceremony where a similar Susan spoke.

The crowd applauded for me as I walked to the platform to join the Lead Ceremonial Director, who was in charge of organizing any and all ceremonies.

"This youth has taken the biggest role for society. He has spent hours, days working to make sure that society will remain at the highest possible standards. Please say a few words, after I induct you," she said monotonously as if she did not care about what she was saying.

"Thank you," I said with a big smile.

"Repeat after me please," she said.

"I hereby promise that I will be an honest and loyal Chief Elder. I will honor The Code and make the necessary changes," she said.

"I promise that I will be a loyal and honest Chief Elder. I will make and honor The Code," I said. I was so nervous that remembering one short sentence was nearly impossible. The crowd cheered when I finished speaking.

"Members of society, I now introduce the Chief Elder," she said as she stepped aside to let me stand at the podium. It was shaped with perfection and its color was solid.

"Welcome everyone. I am very honored to inherit an occupation that is so meaningful to each of you. In our history, the Chief Elder is the member of society that is responsible to ensure a bright future for the entire society. Every day since the Occupation Ceremony, I have worked with the former Chief Elder. He has trained me to be the best member of society I possibly can be. Amongst many topics, I have specifically learned the art of making choices, that can and may affect many lives. So, I will begin the story with choices.

"Two nights ago, I went to sleep expecting the following day to be full of learning. Instead, I woke up unable to find the Chief Elder. I searched in various locations until I heard the four bell rings, and at that time I realized what had happened... and at that very time, I knew that I had to take charge and maintain control... I knew... that I had to do one thing in the coming weeks... improve the lives of which you live ..." I said as the crowd cheered.

"Now I have always wanted things to be different. It is my goal to make some necessary changes. As I have been aging, I have noticed a lack of expansion. I know from my experiences with the Chief Elder that there are other societies out there, past the wall. It is my goal to explore and find our neighbors, share our practices and possibly learn new things," I said. I noticed a lot of people cheering throughout my statement.

"The next objective is a name. It is difficult to live in a society where names are nonexistent. Names allow a culture to be diverse. Names allow each person to be unique. Names allow interactions between members that have a purpose. Names... allow us to live easier. Without names, I am not any different than you, or you, and we want diversity. In other past societies that I have seen, when bad times came, people were mistreated. They were stripped of everything they had to live for including their names. Even though you may like life without names, you have never experienced life with names," I said.

The crowd cheered again.

"Most importantly I want ... I request that you stand for what you believe. It's a new concept, but having your opinions are vital for success ... Success and change! Thank you," I said proudly with a ton of emotion. The whole event seemed like a huge rally.

I had finished my speech flawlessly. The entire crowd stood up and cheered. I knew that society could be better, because I had seen better societies when I was with the Chief Elder. I was also beginning to notice that society as one was becoming more emotional and expressive.

The crowd cheered for a few minutes as I walked off the stage and right to my family, so I could see what they thought about my speech. I then noticed the small flying object with the camera being lowered out of the air.

"You did amazing," my mom said proudly.

"Well done son," my father said.

"That was really amazing," my sister said.

"I think that those ideas you pointed out are very good to look into," my mother said.

"I was thinking that these new concepts would be a good starting point, because the past Chief Elder did not make many changes," I said.

"Well he left that for you," my mom said.

"Indeed, he did...indeed, he did," I said.

Chapter Twenty-Five

Back at headquarters Susan was overwhelmed with what the pawn wanted to do with his power, she just never saw it coming.

Her speech with the president had gone as planned. It drummed up some publicity, some positive publicity for Susan and her experiment. She had hoped that the president enjoyed his quick trip to the headquarters.

"Alright I'm really glad that this video is done," Susan said.

"You rocked it," John said.

"Now let's see what this kid has dreamt up," Susan said.

That was just before the boy gave the speech.

"Oh, looks like we have a lot of changes coming," Commander said.

"I think maybe too many," Susan said.

"I bet you are regretting that device," Commander said.

"Not quite yet, it has given him some exposure. But I did not expect the thing to influence him so much," Susan said.

"Well it was a risk, we will see if it pays off," Derek said.

Location - Society

Over the duration since I had begun my occupation as the Deathmaster, we had never prepared a member of society. The Deathmaster taught me the process and showed me books, but we never got the chance to actually carry out the process.

It was the day after my brother became the Chief Elder.

It came as a surprise to myself and the society. Nobody expected an event of that nature to occur so soon. My brother was clearly caught off guard by the passing, but he wanted to make changes.

I woke up my normal time, prepared for the new day, ate, spoke with my parents. It was all the same, possibly a slight variation in the topic of our conversation.

"Hello mother and father," I said.

"Hello honey," they both said in unison and sounded like stereo.

"What do you think about him being the Chief Elder?" I asked. My parents knew who I was referring to when I spoke. There was one thing my brother and I both agreed with, having names. I did not like calling my brother "him" or "brother." I felt that we should have a name, but as a member of society I knew I couldn't voice my opinions openly.

"I was stunned by this occurrence," my dad said.

"It has never happened, but also nobody ever put thought into it happening," my mother said.

"Same," I said.

"You will likely prepare his remains."

"Oh yeah! I have never seen or done the process in person yet!"

"You sound excited."

"Well I do not know what to expect."

"Don't worry everything will be alright."

"The first time for everything is always a challenge, or even uncomfortable. After that it gets easier," my father said.

"Well shall we embark to a new day?" my mother asked.

"We shall," I said.

We got into our rac, and my mother drove me to my occupation. Along the way I thought about my brother. I always wondered what he did with the device and what other societies look like. Maybe it would be better not to see them, but I had never seen them. I also wondered what he planned to change. I was also a bit nervous about possibly preparing the Chief Elder, because he was the symbol of our society for as long as I could recall.

"Well here you are. Have a great day," my mother said.

"Thank you! I will see you later," I said.

I got out of the rac and went inside.

"Hello," I said to the same secretary. She was always sitting in the same position with the same smile on her face. I could never figure out if her smile was real.

"How are you on this bright beautiful day?" she asked.

⧗   The King's Pawn

"I'm doing fine. How about you?" I asked.

"I too am very good," she said.

I had arrived a little early because I thought that representing my family was very important, so image was huge.

"Please wait as you are early," she said.

"Alright," I said.

I waited in the same room almost every day. I knew that when I became the Deathmaster, I would make sure to let allow my assistant to arrive early. A few minutes later, I was called to the back.

"Thank you for waiting. The Deathmaster is ready," she said.

"Thank you," I said. I no longer needed to be guided to the Deathmaster's office because I knew where it was located. The room where the passed were prepared was separate from the office.

He was sitting at his desk, looking the same as always.

"Hello, how are you?" I asked.

"I am fine, how about yourself?"

"I'm good also," I said.

He always told me what we would be doing for the day after we greeted each other.

"So today, we will prepare the former Chief Elder. This is a very high honor to prepare any member of status. So, we will make sure to do our best," he said.

"But I have never prepared remains before," I said.

"I am aware. There is a first for everything, I will help guide you through this," he said.

"Alright," I said.

"We will also have to determine the cause of passage before we prepare the remains," he said.

"How do we do that?" I asked.

"We have to analyze many different factors. Everything from heart attack, to passage of time, to infections, the list goes on," he said.

"Oh, that sounds difficult," I said.

"It is not difficult, but it has its challenges as does everything," he said.

"I am ready to face those challenges," I said.

"Fantastic! Prepare your gloves and come into the room," he said.

I walked into the room and the remains of the Chief Elder were on a table. It was a horrific sight that scared me. I was not prepared to see the remains on a table. The best description of what I saw was just disturbing. I had never seen remains before, let alone that of the former Chief Elder.

"The first thing we shall do is an external examination. We are looking for external causes of passing," he said.

"Oh, sure alright," I said hesitantly. The one thing that particularly made me uncomfortable was the fact that his eyes were open, and staring at the same spot.

"Shall we shut his eyes?" I asked. The Deathmaster turned around so fast, I nearly missed him.

"Don't shut the eyelids!" he said emotionally. That was the first time he ever showed real emotion or tone of voice.

"Alright, they are bothering me though," I said.

"Me too, but we must examine the eyes," he said.

The whole process was very graphic. From examining the stomach to the brain, everything was disturbing. We had to find what caused the elder to pass, and we were having a very difficult time.

"Since we cannot find any causes, we will take blood samples and test them for unnatural components. I am sure we will not find any because there are no resources available to general society potent enough to cause someone to pass," he said as he was preparing a needle to draw blood.

"Now that the easier tasks are complete, we now start the very rigorous process," he said.

"I thought this was rigorous," I said.

"Not at all, you did not assist me at all, so making an assumption is not ideal right now," he said. I did not know what to respond.

"We will not look at the organs by hand, not visually. We, the two of us, will dissect each one to find a cause of passing," he said.

I was very hesitant to touch the remains. I was already horrified by the whole process. The remains looked like some organism found the remains in the wild. There was blood all over myself and the Deathmaster. The abdomen was cut open to expose the organs. The odor was sickening.

⧗   The King's Pawn

"Now please take these scalpels, and make an incision first to the heart, we have to divide it into two even pieces," he said. I approached the remains, so close I could see every detail.

"No I cannot, I can't," I said. I knew that youth were not to deny authority without making a first attempt.

"You can," he said.

"Fine," I said as I took the scalpels.

I looked into the stomach region at the heart. I made an incision and blood exploded out of the tiny cut. I could tell that the Deathmaster was expecting the blood, because he stepped back when I was about to make the cut.

"Ew!" I screamed as blood covered me. Luckily we had shields that covered our faces, blocking our faces from the blood splatter.

"There are things that happen unexpectedly, this is one of them," he said.

"You knew, because you stepped back right before I made the incision," I said.

"It's alright. I expected your reaction, it is perfectly normal. You will learn from experience," he said. He continued to cut the heart as more blood gushed out.

"What is this object above us?" I asked. I was referring to the circular object hanging from the ceiling. It was not a light, because it did not increase the brightness in the room.

"Ah yes, the camera. It is part of our occupation to document our processes. The camera is taking photos and videos of the remains and each organ, so we do not have to attempt to take photographs," he said.

In reality, the camera was connected to a monitor at headquarters. The video and photo files were being saved to a hard drive to use as forensic evidence.

"Oh alright," I said.

"Come examine this along with me," he said. He had the heart in his hands, as he was inspecting it. I took a step closer to him as he requested.

"There is something unusual with this heart. Take time and tell me what you notice," he said.

I examined the heart that was still dripping with blood. I found the heart interesting, but still unsettling. The only difference about this heart was the red hue. Each organ had a very unique hue, different from that of the society. The heart was very red, but not like the regular heart is.

"I am noticing a darker hue of red," I said.

"Ah perfect! So, what does that mean?" he asked.

"Well it means that something caused irritation in the heart that caused a discoloration," I said.

"Very good, but what would cause this elder to pass?" He asked.

"A lack of blood from the arteries?" I asked.

"Well we have to answer that proposition. You know where to look," he said.

"The coronary arteries," I said.

I found the arteries and cut them open. They appeared normal.

"They are in perfect condition," I said.

"I cannot believe this! All of the signs for a heart attack, but one thing is missing, the coronary arteries are not damaged," he said surprised.

"What do we do about that?" I asked.

"I am at a loss of words, I have never experienced a passing with characteristics like this," he said.

"What do you assume caused the passing?" I asked.

"Well I ... I ... I don't know. He didn't pass of a heart attack. Everything else is fine. I am just puzzled," he said.

"Well we have the blood tests to wait for," I said.

"Very true," he said. "In this situation, we are dealing with the Chief Elder, so we do not have enough time to simply wait for the blood to return. We have to come to a conclusion, since there is not an obvious cause, I will make an assumption," he said.

"What is the cause?" I asked.

"Heart related contributions, unknown cause of passing," he said.

"So, what do you tell the society?" I asked.

"I tell them what is true, which is an unknown cause," he said.

"Do you think that the blood may expose a different cause?" I asked.

"Not at all. A blood test has never told us something we didn't already know. In other societies blood often does tell something, but because no chemicals or substances are available to us, there is not anything like that," he said.

Chapter Twenty-Six

Susan had a busy week and it was not done. The only eyes watching over society were that of Susan King. It was rare for Susan to take a night shift, because she was too lazy to deal with watching society all night. She gave everyone the night off, a very rare occasion for workers.

She was focused on the camera in the Chief Elders bedroom. She watched as he got up and went to drink some water from the glass left on the table. A while later, he was having a hard time breathing, and then he died.

Susan smiled and picked up the phone.

"Yes, report into work immediately!" Susan said.

About thirty minutes later, John and Derek and the Commander arrived.

"Welcome," Susan said.

"Why did you call us in?" the Commander asked.

"The Chief Elder just died!" Susan said as if she was surprised.

"What! He was supposed to live a few more years!" John said.

"I guess not," Susan said.

Derek chuckled. Susan gave Derek the evil eye. He apologized.

"Well now we have to watch what the boy does," Susan said.

"Indeed," Derek said.

"We have to release this to the media asap!" Susan said.

Two Days Later

"Breaking news out of Nevada tonight. Reporting from Nevada is our very own Nancy Anders.

"Nancy Anders here outside the infamous King's Pawn experiment in Nevada. Earlier today, an unexpected tragedy happened. The death of the Chief Elder, who was the head of the society. The cause of death is unknown as of right now, but old age and heart problems are the leading factor. King said quote 'The Chief Elder passed away last night. We do not know what the cause of passing, death was, but old age is likely a cause.' King will likely address the media in the morning. Nancy Anders reporting," Nancy said.

The story made national news, and every news station and newspaper published a story about the "tragedy."

Susan would address the media the following morning.

"Welcome everyone. I will make this quick. As you likely already know, a tragedy has struck my experiment. A few days ago, the Chief Elder passed away. It is a turning point in my experiment as the Chief Elder is a vital position. I cannot state how the death will affect my experiment, but I can tell you it has a great impact. The causes are natural and I can promise that we will not be stopped by this. I have no comment on what has been concluded as the cause of death, but it has been determined. Thank you," Susan said. She knew what really happened.

Location- Society

In the first week of being Chief Elder, the boy had already made some changes to The Code. He attempted to make the society as similar to the other ones he had experienced during training. Many things needed to be changed for the better. He had unlimited power as Chief Elder, which could potentially be catastrophic.

I wanted to find out how the Chief Elder passed. I did not believe the report that claimed heart related causes. I had not touched the bedroom where he slept that night. I assumed that the sleeping room was a good place to look. When I walked in, the sleeping mat remained a mess, the pillows out of order. I did not know where to begin, but the glass on the table was my first object. The Chief Elder always had water at night. The glass had not been touched since the night he passed.

I inspected the glass and it looked a little bit different than the others. This one was not shaped perfectly, but rather a square with rounded edges. I looked past the glass. The next place I checked was the medical cabinet. The Chief Elder was elderly and took many medical care squares that kept him in good shape.

I wanted to see if he possibly took the wrong medicine.

There were six bottles, but he only took one pill at night. The bottle had a very long word that I couldn't pronounce on it. I looked inside and saw a pill. It did not look right. It was white and rather large.

The Chief Elder possessed a device that would determine the chemical makeup of any substance inserted. The Chief Elder never showed me how to use it, but I saw him use it. He had told me that the device used different chemicals to dissolve the sample. Based on which chemicals dissolved the sample, the device determined the sample.

I went downstairs to the office where the device was located. It was on a table, ready for use. I decided to grab the bottle with the pill and bring it downstairs, not before I took a picture of the pill.

I turned the machine on and waited for the "Insert Sample" logo to appear. After about sixteen seconds, the logo appeared. I poured the pill into the funnel and waited. The machine took a few minutes to accurately determine the sample. During the time I could hear the machine working, because it made odd sounds.

After four minutes, the tiny piece of paper printed out. I could not believe what I saw on the paper.

I knew immediately that he did not pass of heart related problems, no it was far worse. In fact, I nearly screamed when I saw the tiny piece of paper.

I knew what I needed to do next ...

Chapter Twenty-Seven

I took the slip of paper and immediately sat down. I needed to gather thoughts to ensure that I did not do wrong actions. I wanted to find out more information, so I immediately went to my mother for help. She was always willing to give me advice.

I got in the blue rac and immediately drove over to my home. I went much faster than allowed, but I wanted answers. I arrived after some time at the home, but my mother's rac was missing. The problem was I did not know where her occupation was. I needed to go find out where she was, but I was running out of time.

"Rac rac, can you hear me?" I asked. I was hoping that the voice that always spoke to me would respond when I spoke to it.

A few seconds passed ... no response. More time passed and still nothing.

"Why! Why! This won't work!" I said. I didn't realize that I was speaking what I was thinking.

"Um ... hello what do you need?" the voice asked.

"Where is my mother's occupation?" I asked.

"Searching ..." the voice said. After about a minute it responded again.

"She, she ... currently she is located at the Chief Elders LOO," the voice said.

"That cannot be! I just came from there!" I said.

"It appears as if she is inside at the moment," the voice said.

"Thank you!" I said.

"Why mother why?" I asked at the volume of a whisper.

I began the drive back to the home. I was very confused as to what my mother was doing.

The voice was truthful, my mother's rac was positioned near the home. I wanted to remain undetected to figure out what she was doing at the home. I approached the front door, and it was ajar. I opened it as silently as possible, again so my mother didn't know I had arrived. I stood outside the door and I could hear her voice.

"The pill, the one pill, where is it! I can't find it!" she said as she moved around.

I peeked inside and she was in the office near the device that I had used to get the paper.

"Oh my ... I hope he didn't," she said.

"Hope he didn't do what?" I asked as I entered the home. I could tell she did not realize my presence because she was startled to the point that she jumped when I spoke.

"What are you doing back so soon?" she asked nervously.

"I got a little help from a voice," I said.

"That's how," she said.

"Now answer me a question please. What are you doing?" I asked.

"Well ... I ... am," she said stuttering.

"It appears you are looking for this," I said as I held up the small piece of paper.

"You didn't ... it can't be!" she said shuddering. "No please no, this cannot be," she continued.

"What is wrong?" I asked.

"Nothing, nothing at all," she said.

"Where is the pill? The pill in the bottle?" she asked me.

"I used that machine to tell what the pill was made of," I said.

"Oh God, please no!" she said extremely worried.

"How?" I asked.

"Later," she said.

"You lied, didn't you? You knew about this but why, why did you betray my trust?" I asked.

My mother started to tear up.

"I don't know! It's not easy, to lie to my own son!" she said in tears.

"But why? Why would you lie to me?" I asked.

"I just wanted this to all work out the right way! It is vital," she said sobbing by this time.

"But what is the importance of this pill?" I asked.

"That, I cannot explain to you, but you will likely discover the real truth," she said. She was trying to hold her emotions back

"What do you mean real? Are we not real?" I asked.

"We are real, but you will discover what I mean sooner or later," she said.

"Now! I want to find out the truth now," I said firmly

My mother was still tearing up.

"Wait, one more thing … How did cyanide get in society?" I asked. My mother's facial expressions changed so much. She looked worried and still very nervous.

"I do not know, but you have the power to discover the power to do whatever you wish in your life, whether it be inside or outside of society," she said as she ran out of the home.

I had to figure out how cyanide got into the society, because it was only available in other societies, or so I was told.

The Next Day

I wanted to make a change to our society, exploration. My mother's words gave me a passion to see these other societies, these other seemingly foreign places. I went to the center of society to address the members of society.

"Welcome again everyone!" I said. They all responded aloud.

"Today I came here to speak to you about an immediate change I am making. When I was in training with the Chief Elder, he spoke of other societies, each with unique people and traditions.

"We will send out a team of explorers later today to find our boundaries and report back to us. Together as one, we will work and fight to discover and reach new heights and achieve greater things. I want to assure you that there are other people living outside of our society. Their societies are much different than ours, but the people are able to live better lives.

"I am requesting a flying object to be used right at this moment in time. Fly it to the boundary so you the members can see that I am indeed telling you the truth ... while ... while we wait ... Thank you thank you for the applause ... Now, our next goal is to rewrite The Code. I am aware of the life you live, as I lived it just days ago, and I am also aware that it is very boring and pointless," I said.

The crowd cheered, all but one member who was rebellious.

"Our life is great you liar!" he screamed. This was the first time any member ever spoke out against the controlling force.

"One rule I am adding, is that you will not be allowed to speak against me. Doing so will result in a severe punishment. I will not tolerate any rebellious actions," I said. The crowd turned towards the man.

"I am sorry. I apologize," he said.

"Normally I would give forgiveness, but forgiveness is a form of weakness and I will not express any weakness. This man will serve you all an example of what not to do! I want him in the Condemning Station for as long as he lives," I said. I did not want the man to be harmed, but I worried about a retaliation that other societies faced in the past.

"The flying object is very close to the border, so I will show you the live view behind me," I said. After about two minutes of watching the flying object fly, the wall came into view.

"Now that the object has reached its destination, we shall see the boundary on the screen," I said. The crowd gasped in a stunned way.

"As you can see, we are surrounded, but we shall rise to overcome the thickest of walls, the highest barriers, nothing will stop us from our goal!" I said. The crowd went wild.

"What about names?" someone shouted. It was interesting how more and more society members were breaking their shells.

"As I was about to state ... Names ... I have decided to present you with names from other societies to choose from. You will then report to one of my officers at my office to have your name recorded. In three days, anyone without a name will be an outsider and considered an act against the governing body," I said. The crowd cheered very loudly.

It was hard for me to say the next part of the speech.

"As for myself, and for anyone of our society, this will be the first time you will have names. What I am about to state is also a historical benchmark of our ongoing history," I said. The crowd went silent.

"On this day in history, the first member of our society was given a name. I am Kyle," I said.

The crowd did not know how to respond. For me, I had heard the name Kyle from training, and I liked it because of its simplicity. I wanted simple because for a powerful position simple sometimes worked out better.

"One more thing ... the name Kyle is forbidden for any other member of society. Do not find out what the punishment is ... " I said. The crowd cheered and began to stand up.

On the screen behind me, my name was printed in big red letters, I AM K-Y-L-E. I also noticed my family in the audience cheering proudly.

I got off of the platform and went straight over to my family. They were proud that I was making changes.

"Hi mother, and father!" I said.

"Hello son," my father said.

"My name is Kyle!" I said.

"Hello Kyle," he said.

I noticed my mother started to cry.

"Hello Kyle," my sister said.

"Hello! I saw a name for you ... Brittany, I think it fits you well," I said.

"It is beautiful," she said.

"Do you think you will choose that name?" I asked.

"Yes, I will definitely," she said.

"Well honey ... you are doing great in your position. I understand how difficult this is," my mother said.

"My name is Amy," my mother said.

"Amy, I like my role, being able to make changes," I said.

Location - Headquarters

Susan King was being faced with many difficult decisions. As the boy was making more changes, she became more and more worried. The experiment was slowly getting out of control.

"Susan what do we do about the boy and his exploration?" the Commander asked.

Over the last year, Susan's mental stability had changed a bit. She was becoming increasingly stressed by her experiment. Her choices and requests had become more lazy. She was playing the role of the crowd watching the fight, not the person preventing the fight.

"We wait and see," Susan said.

"But Susan this boy literally wants to overcome our boundary!" Commander exclaimed.

"Well you can just quit if you don't like my rules!" Susan said.

"I won't quit! This could be a terrible mistake on your end! Don't let fifteen years go to waste!" he said.

"Then what do you think I should do?" Susan said.

"Susan please calm down! We need to gather ourselves professionally!" John said from his office.

"We watch," Susan said.

Luckily nothing happened that put the experiment at risk ... nothing yet.

Location - Experiment

I decided to have more rallies to talk to the people. The people liked my ideas, I had not heard anything bad about me.

Two days had passed since I gave the speech about names. I was writing a plan to get people, a lot of them, to join my side and break through the boundaries. I decided to order a meeting with the Board of Elders.

"Welcome all," I said.

"Welcome Kyle," they replied.

"Today, we are here to discuss exploration. I will tell you what I do know. There is a big obstruction, a wall, about thirty miles distance away from the center of the society. It is strong and our drones don't work past it, so I cannot see very far. I want us to get past it somehow. At any and all costs, we will get past the wall. I want to hear your thoughts and ideas," I said.

"Well Kyle, that would be considered a rebellion against authority, you just spoke against it. So that would be the first problem," an elder said.

"Agreed," another elder said.

"I failed to notice that. I will either change the rule or make it seem as if the act isn't a rebellion. It isn't written yet, because I did just mention it," I said.

"Well Kyle, are you trying to take over the society?" an elder asked.

"No. I would never attempt to take over society. I am just the leader, I am not the brain. I just want the best for the body," I said.

"Things like this take a great deal of time. We have to propose a plan, and then carry out said plan," a female elder said.

"Well I want things done as fast as possible. You will just need to propose quickly and carry out quicker," I said.

"Yes master," they said.

"One more thing ... figure out where this came from," I said as I put the paper in the table.

"Why that's impossible! There is no such substance here!" an elder said.

"How did you get this substance?" an elder asked.

"I didn't get it, someone else did, and I think it caused the passing of the Chief Elder!" I said.

"Are you saying a member of society harmed the Chief Elder?" the female elder asked.

"I am saying that someone killed the Chief Elder, and whoever did it will get the most severe punishment," I said.

"We will definitely work immediately to find the source," an elder said.

"Very well then. With that, the meeting is concluded," I said.

After I concluded the meeting, I went back to the home to think about my actions and write down my thoughts. I knew I wanted to get the society to favor me as their leader. I also knew I wanted them to understand and follow my authority. Secretly, the whole idea of exploration was to get past the seemingly invincible walls that surrounded society. Go out, get past the boundaries to discover what there is to be discovered. I had awareness of other societies from training, and I realized that our society seemed irregular, as none of the other societies ran so flawless. I wrote a few words on the paper "find the guilty member." I wanted to find the member who used a poison to harm the Chief Elder. Nothing was going to stop me...

Over time, I scouted out the locations of the very, very tiny cameras. I never figured out how they functioned being so minute. Two of which were in my home, one right above my sitting area. I looked right at the camera and spoke to it.

"I know someone is there ... and nothing will stop me from what I am about to do ... mark my words!"

I had noticed a change in my mental state after I became the Chief Elder. I was more powerful, fearless, emotionless, and a lot more determined.

The Next Day

I woke up very early, after a tough night of little sleep. It was only around five in the morning. That day I set out to rat out the culprit.

At five thirty, I decided to have the announcement, despite most members of society being in a state of sleep. There was a small machine on the desk that would project my voice very loudly upon society, so that everyone could hear it clearly.

"Good morning, rise and shine! Today is a bright beautiful day, as it always is. Today you will all meet at the Center of Society at seven sharp. Please do not be late. Nobody ever is, but still don't be late. We will ask each and every member one question and that is all ... I have finished my announcement. My name is Kyle," I said.

I could hear an echo of my rumbling voice. I hoped that all of the members heard the announcement.

I planned to have the False Machines used to determine if the members were giving out the truth.

7:00 am

I was at the Center of Society just to make sure that everything went as I wanted. There were twelve tables set up, each with a False Machine. Every member of Society was in attendance. I knew it would take all day for the results, but there were three people I wanted to personally administer the test to ... my family.

I searched for my family in the crowds of people lined up silently. After a few minutes of searching, I found my family waiting towards the back of a line.

"Kyle!" my sister said. She spotted me before my mother or father.

"Hello Brittany," I said as I hugged her.

"Hello honey," my mother said. Something about her seemed different. She just looked nervous. She seemed emotional also.

"Hi mother! What is bothering you?" I asked.

"Nothing much. It is tough right now, as things are changing I think," she said warily.

"Well I want to personally administer your exams if that is alright," I said.

"It is," my father said.

"Hello father," I said.

"Hi," he said emotionless. I gave him a hug also.

I led them to the front of the line.

"Can I please administer the next three?" I asked the woman who was asking the question.

"Yes Master Kyle," she said.

"Thank you," I said.

She quickly finished the exam and stood up.

The machines worked fairly simply. There was a heart beat monitor that attaches to one's arm or finger. If the heartbeat sped up, then that member was not telling the truth. If that happened, then the machine would print a paper, that would immediately be given to me.

"I will go first," my sister said.

"Alright," I said as I attached the clip to her finger. I waited about a minute to allow me to see her average heart rate, mainly to base any fluctuation on.

"Answer with yes or no, nothing else. Did you harm the Chief Elder?" I asked.

"No ..." she said. Nothing happened, so she was telling the truth. I could see the tiny horizontal line on the screen relatively flat.

"Good job! You passed! Mother do you want to go next?" I asked.

"Sure, sure I think," she said hesitantly. I could sense she was extremely nervous for the test.

"Answer with yes or no, nothing else. Did you harm the Chief Elder?" I asked.

"No," she said. Again, I waited a little bit to see the screen. Then all of a sudden the line was not flat. I thought that it was a discrepancy, so I asked her a question to test the machine, covering any mistakes.

"Do you drive a white rac?" I asked.

"Yes," she said. The line remained flat, ruling out a mistake.

"Okay ... Did you harm the Chief Elder?" I asked again.

"No," she said. The line moved again. She was not telling the truth. I had a hard time believing the moment. It was the worst moment of realization in my life. I knew right then.

"I need assistance," I said to the woman standing behind me.

"Yes Kyle?" she asked.

"Test my mother again, while I excuse myself," I said.

"Yes master," she said.

I walked away from the lines of people, where I could think about what just happened.

My mother may have harmed the Chief Elder. Why would she do such a thing? But I could not punish her, because she was my mother. If I didn't, then my authority would be weak. I ran back to the line to find her, but she was not there. She was nowhere to be found. I went to the nearest speaker to make my announcement.

"Everyone, find my mother immediately, bring her to me!" I said angrily.

Everyone suddenly began looking for my mother, it caused a bit of a chaos. It took only a minute for her to be turned in to me. The member who turned her in ran away from me as quickly as possible.

"I'm sorry," she said in tears. "I made a mistake! I love you Kyle!"

"Come with me to the home," I said.

Chapter Twenty-Eight

Location - Headquarters

Susan was watching the cameras with the other people who worked for her. She knew what had happened and she was very worried about her future. She did not want to intervene.

"Susan what will we do?" John asked.

"Wait, I do not want to act now," Susan said.

"Susan do you understand what is going on right now?" Commander asked.

"Yes, my experiment," she said.

"No, no, noo! Susan listen carefully! This experiment is failing, and very quickly. You must do something! The last time you didn't do anything, the situation got worse!" Commander exclaimed angrily.

"Susan! If the mother is put in jail, or even killed, then your experiment is worthless and void! Do you understand that? It's over!" Derek asked.

"Yes, I do," she said carelessly.

"Have you lost your mind, or has power gone to your head?" Commander asked.

"Neither, trust me, it will be alright," she said. She really was not at her best mentally, she did not realize the direness of the situation playing out in front of her eyes.

John was very worried, as he should be.

"Susan, we do not trust you! Do you realize you will be charged with murder if he kills his mother?" John asked.

"No, I will not! Nobody has to ever know about it," she said. She would do everything in her power to cover up the death.

"Susan you are losing it again! Please realize what is really happening! Your experiment is on the verge of failure! Failure!!" Commander yelled.

"Alright, alright! I will consider intervening," she yelled back.

"But Susan ..." John said, but he was interrupted by the boy speaking.

"Mother ... my power is at stake! If I forgive you, then they will overcome me!" the boy said. The mother was crying.

"This is the worst thing a son should ever have to experience. I do not want to make a decision, but I have to," the boy said.

"But honey, we can work this out! There can be a better solution! Please I beg!" she pleaded. She was crying, and her son was too. He understood that this conversation would be one of the last the two would ever have.

"Well mother, tell me, what are you hiding!" he demanded loudly.

"Honey I am really sorry! I really should have told you!" she said regretfully.

"Tell me what?" he said.

"Well I cannot tell you, at least not right now!" she said.

"But why? Why cyanide?" he asked.

"Well you were never supposed to find out!" she said. She knew that her big mistake was leaving that one extra pill in the container. The experiment would have continued if it weren't for that pill.

"Well I did, now tell me your secrets!" he said.

"Not right now! If you do not banish me I will tell you!" she said crying.

"Then you will not be banished, you will be the first to climb the wall right now! We will go as a family, just you, Brittany, dad, and myself!" he said.

"I should have thought about this better," she said in tears. "I am sorry!"

"You made an irreversible mistake!" he said.

Susan had grabbed a radio to speak to the guards.

"Do not shoot anything!" Susan exclaimed. "If it is living you will not shoot!"

"Susan, what do we do?" John asked.

"We pray!" Susan said.

About thirty minutes later, the four members of society reached the wall. The boy had tied a large ladder to his blue rac.

"Out!" the boy said to his mother. Everyone but the father was very emotional. Brittney did not know what had happened, until Kyle told her during the trip.

"Please, no please!" the mother said begging.

"Kyle please don't!" Brittany said. She felt terrible that her mother betrayed her kids.

"Well this is a lesson to think before you carry out actions!" he said.

The boy untied the ladder and placed it against the wall, reaching the top.

"I loved you mother and I still do, but this is it!" he said. He knew this was the last moment.

"I love you! I want to say one thing to you two! This isn't real! It is all a fake!" she said.

"What do you mean?" Brittany asked.

"This was all planned!" the mother said.

"I love you mom!" Brittany said emotionally.

"I love you too! Goodbye!" the mother said. She went over and gave Brittany a very long hug, her last hug. Brittany was in tears.

Before she started the climb, she went over to Kyle.

"Honey, I want you to know that I love you and will always love you despite what you believe. You are my son, and I love you!" Amy said. This was the most emotional interaction yet, they both knew they would never again hug or hear each other's words.

The mother began the climb up the ladder. This whole experience was very emotional for the family.

"No don't, please don't!" Susan screamed. She too was emotional at this point. Her life ending more and more as Amy climbed up each rung of the ladder.

"Well, we just told you to intervene!" John said.

All eyes were on Susan King...

"What are you looking at me for?" Susan asked.

⧗   The King's Pawn

"Alright, I am guilty I told the mother to use cyanide! I gave it to her! I confess!" Susan screamed, knowing everything would begin to fall. She was swearing too.

"How could you!? We have trusted you for years!" Derek said.

"Well I have done a lot of things that you would not agree with!" Susan said emotionally.

She picked up her radio to speak to the guards.

"Susan King here do not shoot! Repeat do not shoot!!" Susan yelled.

The voice was faint, but audible.

"Dr. King, on day one you signed a contract to allow us to shoot anything escaping! It said that nothing can override the rule, so I have to shoot," the guard said.

"No! No ... no please no!" Susan screamed. The realization of what Susan did kicked into everyone's mind.

"If it wasn't for that damn pill, this never would have gone wrong. I should have only given one," Susan screamed.

She had forgotten about her rule that told guards to shoot any living soul over the wall.

"Well it's done! Everything is ruined! Say goodbye to each other as it's all ending now!" Susan said.

"What do you mean?" Commander asked.

Susan pointed to the screen. The mother was five rungs away from the top of the wall. Time seemed to pass much slower than it really did for Susan.

"Oh my ..." Derek said.

The mood was hopeless inside the headquarters, as they all realized what was happening.

She was on the last rung, and she blew a kiss to her family. They were an emotional wreck. Amy knew her life would come to an end.

"I love you all!" she said sobbing. She knew that she was going to die. She wanted her children's lives to be better.

She climbed the final rung and looked over the wall at her ending.

She stood up on top of the wall and jumped off with almost no hesitation. There was a guard on the other side with his gun pointed at her. He knew what his orders were.

One shot rang out.

Amy was lying on the ground, slowly losing consciousness, when she uttered her final words.

"Susan, die in a nasty place with people like y..." she muttered.

"That is it! She is gone! It is all over! The experiment failed!" Susan said sobbing. She was throwing items around the headquarters out of rage and regret.

"What just happened?" John asked.

"My life being ruined in one second ... just happened," Susan said. She had a terrible feeling of guilt.

They failed to notice the boy kissing his sister.

"I love you! We will never know the secret, but I want you to join me to find out! Let's climb over this wall!" the boy said to his sister.

"Let's!" she replied emotionally.

The two started to climb up the ladder towards their demise. They did not know that the guard was busy tending to the mother.

They jumped carefully, and the boy sprained his ankle on the jump. They slipped past the guard who could not hear them passing, because he could only hear Susan King screaming in his ear piece.

Had the guard not been occupied, the two children would have been shot also.

The two kids escaped the grounds of the experiment and were in the real world for the first time in fifteen years... unknown to anyone.

Chapter Twenty-Nine

The whole day, Susan was an emotional wreck. Her whole life's work was shattered in a second. John and Derek were also in a state of disbelief. Everyone lost fifteen years of their life. John, Derek and the Commander benefited from the experiment, they made their millions.

The next morning at 9:24, four people exited the grounds of the King's Pawn in a line. The media rushed them, along with the police and security who were permanently stationed there.

"My name is Susan King, and on this day, I have lost everything I had to live for!" she said to the media.

"Dr. King please explain!" a reporter said.

The unexpected appearance was on the news all over the world within five minutes. It was typical for Susan's special reports to give breaking news, but nobody expected her news to be so breaking ...

"On this day, March 16th, the King's Pawn experiment has officially failed! We have reached checkmate! One of the members of our society escaped and was shot dead by one of our guards following protocol," Susan said. She knew what the real truth was, but she was not about to share it.

"What will you do now?" a reporter asked.

"We will attempt to live our lives," John said.

"And I will rot in prison! It is an eternal checkmate! I confess to you right now my crimes! I have nothing to live for! I am guilty of fraud and I orchestrated the murder! Arrest me now!" Susan said. It was to her benefit to confess because she had nothing else to lose, and she hoped that her confession would lower her sentence. She was wrong.

She was immediately handcuffed by two police officers and put into the nearest police car.

"Gentlemen, do you have any comments?" a reporter asked.

"Yes! Do not be afraid to act in a tough situation!" the Commander said.

"And for me! Listen to him! Do not be afraid to act in a fishy situation! Please kids, do not make my mistakes!" Susan said as she was being dragged away. "Do not do what I did!"

"What could have been done to prevent this outcome?" a reporter asked.

"Well, speaking for my colleagues and myself, we should have conducted this experiment honestly and truthfully. Most importantly, our mistake was turning this scientific experiment into a profitable experiment. That is where we started to go downhill," the Commander said.

Breaking news today out of the United States. The largest human experiment on record has officially failed today. Susan King, the leader and creator of the King's Pawn said to media that "the experiment has failed as one of our members was killed" She also confessed to murder and fraud; she has yet to appear in court."

Later that day, Derek would make the only televised interview.

"We have Derek from the King's Pawn here in studio today from Las Vegas, to tell me what happened," the reporter said.

"Yes. Essentially, Dr. King failed to act when the boy wanted to make some changes. Then it all culminated down to the mother being shot by the guard. As for me, my life is over, I have no job and will never have one. I want people to know that we are serious when we say speak up. It caused many people to die, many years wasted, and lives ruined. That's it for me," Derek said.

"Thank you! Sorry about that viewers, but Derek has requested an early release."

Nobody noticed the two teenage children roaming the desert near the headquarters ...

"We need to get as far from here as possible and find a new society to live in," Kyle said.

A Few Days Later

The event was all over the news, not only in America.

People were still getting their heads wrapped around the fact that the King's Pawn failed.

Susan was arrested. She was going to be moved to a large Federal penitentiary. She was temporarily put in a jail just outside of Las Vegas. Susan did not like the jail life and she was only at a small jail.

The news broke out of thin air.

"We have breaking news out of Las Vegas this morning. Former head of the King's Pawn experiment, Susan King has just been reported as an escaped convict after she was discovered missing from her jail cell late last night. Her experiment failed a few days ago due to her fraudulent actions, so she may be trying to get out of the country. If you see her, do not confront her, but rather call 911 as quickly as you can!" the reporter said.

Susan was in a getaway car headed north on the expressway headed out of Las Vegas with a driver she knew. When she found out that the two children were not in the experiment, she knew that they must have escaped. They were her top priority...

"I must find those children!" she said loudly.

The King's Pawn